A BRUTAL  VE
LAWMAN .   CUE

JOHN McCAIN—The rugged U.S. marshal is hand-picked by the government to lead an unthinkably dangerous rescue into the very heart of a band of guerrillas. It will take cagey planning, split-second timing, and enough courage to face a remorseless terrorist—and win.

DUNCAN CAMPBELL—The distinguished U.S. secretary of war has been smoothing out tensions with Mexico's generalissimo. But now he finds himself and his family at the center of an international crisis—and the key players in a desperate race across Mexico.

LUCY CAMPBELL—The secretary's beautiful, blond, twenty-two-year-old daughter discovers that she has been captured twice: first by the vicious terrorists—and then by the charms of the handsome marshal who comes to her rescue.

JOSÉ GRISTO—The fierce, heartless leader of the Guatemalan guerrillas, he vows that either the captured Guatemalans will be freed from their jail cell—or the secretary of war and his family will pay the penalty of cruel, painful death.

The Stagecoach Series
Ask your bookseller for the books you have missed

STAGECOACH STATION 47:
JUÁREZ

Hank Mitchum

BANTAM BOOKS
NEW YORK · TORONTO · LONDON · SYDNEY · AUCKLAND

JUÁREZ
*A Bantam Book / published by arrangement with
Book Creations, Inc.
Bantam edition / May 1990*

*Produced by Book Creations, Inc.
Lyle Kenyon Engel: Founder*

ISBN 0-553-28477-0

Published simultaneously in the United States and Canada

*Bantam Books are published by Bantam Books, a division of Bantam
Doubleday Dell Publishing Group, Inc. Its trademark, consisting of
the words ''Bantam Books'' and the portrayal of a rooster, is Registered
in U.S. Patent and Trademark Office and in other countries. Marca
Registrada. Bantam Books, 666 Fifth Avenue, New York, New York 10103.*

PRINTED IN THE UNITED STATES OF AMERICA

RAD   0 9 8 7 6 5 4 3 2 1

JUÁREZ

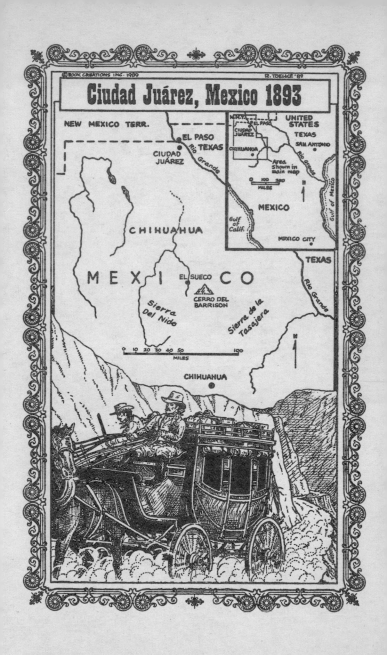

Prologue

A flash of blue-white lightning split the black sky, briefly illuminating the Mexican border town of Ciudad Juárez. A steady, drenching rain had been falling since dusk, lashed by gusts of wind sweeping down from the north over the Rio Grande and pelting anyone venturing through the muddy streets.

A lone figure, his hat pulled low and water running off his slicker, stepped from the alley beside the plush Buena Vista Hotel and rounded the corner. Climbing the smooth marble steps, he entered the hotel's lobby and stood just inside the door for a moment, his ebony eyes taking in the crowd of people milling about. Then, removing his hat and shaking the water from it, he made his way across the lobby to the waist-high partition that separated the adjoining dining room.

Oblivious to the gay music of the mariachi band strolling among the diners, Mario Cuello gazed slowly from table to table until he found the familiar face of Generalissimo Fernando Velásquez. Judging from the expression on the silver-haired generalissimo's face and his expansive gestures, he was greatly enjoying the sumptuous dinner he was having with people who were clearly *norteamericanos*. Smiling to himself, Cuello automatically hitched up the gun belt under his slicker and then sat in a nearby overstuffed chair. All he could do now was wait.

1

Generalissimo Fernando Velásquez, a stout, swarthy man in his sixties, was Mexico's top military official. He cut an imposing figure in his bone-white uniform bedecked with gold piping, gold-trimmed epaulets on his shoulders, and a chestful of silver and gold medals decorated with brightly colored ribbons.

Seated directly across the candlelit table from the generalissimo was the United States secretary of war, Duncan Campbell. The secretary was a distinguished-looking, handsome man in his early fifties with a thick head of salt-and-pepper hair—of which his wife had jokingly said of late that it was more salt than pepper—who seemed as though he had been born to be a government official.

To Duncan Campbell's right sat his wife, Patricia, whose poise and dignity reflected her position in life. In her late forties and still a beauty, her medium-brown hair was lightly and becomingly streaked with gray, and her still-curvaceous figure was not much different from that of her daughter, Lucy's.

The blond, vivacious Lucy sat to the secretary's left. Like her mother, the twenty-two-year-old woman was of medium height, and her beauty had captured the attention of several young men in the restaurant—as had her sky-blue eyes and her dazzling smile.

Also in the party were the Campbells' long-time friends William and Belinda Stanford and their fifteen-year-old son, Merrill. During the past three days, Patricia and Lucy had been visiting with the Stanfords in El Paso, Texas, across the Rio Grande from Juárez, while President Grover Cleveland's war secretary had been engaged in official talks with the generalissimo.

A recent Mexican uprising in Texas had strained relations between the neighboring countries, but the three days of over-the-table talks had restored the good rapport between the United States and Mexico, and with the meetings successfully concluded, Generalissimo Velásquez was hosting the exquisite dinner for the Americans. The

Stanfords had been graciously included as a gesture of farewell, for they were scheduled to leave by train from El Paso for Washington, D.C., the next day, May 5, 1893.

When the meal was finished, Velásquez rose to his feet with a glass of wine in his hand and said in heavily accented English, "If I may, I would like to toast my American visitors."

Secretary Campbell stood as well, graciously responding, "And I propose a toast to our host. I feel confident that as a result of the talks we have just concluded, Mexico and the United States will once again enjoy amicable relations."

Smiling broadly, the generalissimo declared expansively, "*Sí!* That is my wish as well, Señor Campbell—that we and our neighbors to the north always have amicable relations!"

After trading polite niceties, everyone stood up, and the generalissimo bowed to the women and shook hands with the men. "If you will excuse me, I have noticed some of my fellow dignitaries on the other side of the dining room, and I must speak with them."

"Certainly, Generalissimo, and thank you for your delightful hospitality," Duncan Campbell rejoined. After watching the Mexican walk away, the secretary turned to his friends and suggested, "The evening is young yet, and being tied up in these meetings every day hasn't allowed me to spend much time with you. How about coming up to our suite for a little while?"

The Stanfords looked at each other and then nodded. "It would be our pleasure, Duncan," William replied. "Let's go."

Chatting merrily as they passed through the hotel lobby and mounted the sweeping curved staircase to the second floor, the two families were unaware that they were being followed by Mario Cuello. They topped the stairs and started down the hall, and Duncan Campbell pulled the key from his pocket when the group reached his suite. Unlocking the door, he pushed it open and, with a sweep of his hand, smiled at the Stanfords and told them, "Please enter our humble abode."

After everyone had entered, the war secretary pocketed the key and quietly closed the door. Catching up with the others, he was about to ask them to sit down when a bedroom door burst open and three swarthy men with pistols drawn barged into the room. Almost simultaneously, three more charged in from the other bedroom.

"Everybody stay right where you are!" snarled the meanest-looking one of the lot.

The Americans were in complete shock.

"What's the meaning of this?" the secretary finally demanded.

The leader did not answer, but instead he asked, "Which of you are the Campbells?"

Anger crawled through Duncan Campbell. Face flushed, he snapped, "That is none of your business!"

The leader's mouth hardened, and he slashed at Campbell's face with the barrel of his revolver. Campbell threw up a forearm, partially blocking the blow, although the tip of the barrel nicked his nose.

One of the other men leapt beside Campbell and jammed his gun into the secretary's ribs. "Answer my friend's question, *gringo!*" he growled. "Who among you are the Campbells?"

The secretary's nose was trickling blood and his arm was throbbing with pain. As he pulled out a handkerchief and held it to his nose, he realized it was foolish to try to fight these men. "I am Duncan Campbell," he admitted. "And these two ladies are my wife and my daughter. Now, what do you want?"

The leader made a quick motion with his head. While several of the men held guns on the group, the others handcuffed the Campbells.

Lucy's anguished face showed the mixture of fear and confusion that she was feeling. "Father . . ." she breathed, her trembling voice rising in pitch.

"Try to stay calm, honey," Campbell replied evenly, pressing more composure into his voice than he was really feeling.

As the Stanfords looked on in fright, Patricia Campbell moved protectively close to her daughter, never once taking her eyes off the vicious leader.

At that moment the door to the hallway opened, and Mario Cuello entered. All eyes turned toward him as he held the door slightly ajar and said to the leader, "There is no one in the hall, José. Are you ready?"

"Not yet," replied the grim-faced man. "You keep watch."

Cuello nodded, turned around, and pulled the door almost closed. Pressing his face close to the jamb, he watched the hallway.

Desperation was on Duncan Campbell's face and in his voice as he said to the leader, "I don't know who you are or what you're planning to do, but my family and I are here as official guests of Generalissimo Fernando Velásquez. For such an outrageous act as this, you and these men will bring down the wrath of your own government on your heads."

The rough-looking leader laughed insolently and mocked, "But we are not Mexicans—we are Guatemalans! I am guerrilla chief José Gristo, and you and your family are being abducted in the name of Guatemala's *presidente*, Enrique Cresada.

"For what reason?" Campbell demanded angrily, dabbing the bloody handkerchief to his nose with his shackled hands. "I assume it has something to do with my governmental position."

"It does," Gristo replied flatly. "But that is all you will ask me. Do not ask any more questions. You will find out the reason later. Right now, we must leave."

In the momentary silence that followed the guerrilla's words, the low rumble of thunder and the rain beating against the windows of the suite could be clearly heard.

"Well, whatever it is that you want me for," Campbell

countered levelly, "my wife and daughter are innocent bystanders. They are not at all involved in the workings of our government. Please. Let them stay here with our friends."

Gristo gave the secretary a stony look and replied in a voice that was cold and malicious, "There will be no friends for them to stay with, *señor*. These people must die. We can leave no witnesses behind."

Suddenly it seemed as though the storm were raging inside the room. Belinda Stanford gasped loudly, while her husband, in an act born of desperation, pushed his wife and son toward the door and then lunged at the guerrilla who stood closest to him, attempting to grab his revolver. The guerrilla whipped the gun out of reach and clouted William Stanford on the head with it.

As Stanford was staggering from the blow, knives were pulled from sheaths and, while José Gristo held his gun on the Campbells, his men swiftly stabbed the Stanfords to death. Lucy screamed loudly, and her mother reached up with her shackled hands and turned her daughter's head away from the horror. Duncan Campbell reflexively went after the killers, but Gristo leapt in front of him, pointing the gun between his eyes, and Campbell checked his move.

Enraged by Lucy's continuous screams, one of the guerrillas stepped beside her and slapped her savagely across the face. "Shut up!" he hissed.

The young woman staggered backward and fell over a chair, tumbling to the floor, and Patricia immediately went to her and tried to comfort her. Lucy looked at her mother with a face twisted in disbelief. "Tell me this isn't really happening," she whispered. "Surely this is a nightmare." She began to whimper. "Oh, Mother, I'm so frightened!"

Before Patricia could respond, one of the guerrillas grabbed Lucy's arm and forced her to her feet. José

Gristo turned to Mario Cuello and asked, "Is anyone coming? Someone might have heard the screams."

Cuello widened the door, stuck his head out and then pulled it back in. "No one in sight," he replied with relief.

"All right," Gristo snapped at the Campbells, "let's go!"

The Campbells moved obediently toward the door, unwilling to risk the further wrath of their cold-blooded captors. As they reached the door, the Americans glanced back at the lifeless, bloody bodies of their friends lying in grotesque positions on the floor.

Lucy hesitated at the doorway, silent tears streaming down her face. But her father touched her arm, urging softly, "Come on, honey. Do as they say."

Mario Cuello kept a lookout toward the main staircase while the captives were led down the back stairs and outside into the alley.

Windswept rain lashed the group as they sloshed through ankle-deep mud toward a dark huddle of horses. One of the animals nickered and bobbed its head when lightning flashed and illuminated the alley for a few seconds. From the saddlebags of three of the horses, the guerrillas pulled slickers, putting them on the Campbells once the prisoners were mounted. Mario Cuello then raced up from the back of the hotel, informing José Gristo that as far as he could tell, no one had seen them.

As the Guatemalans and their captives rode away into the night, a jagged bolt of lightning slashed the sky. It was immediately answered by a sharp, angry clap of thunder—counterpoint to the brutal event that had just taken place.

Chapter One

On a wooded hillside a few miles north of Austin, Texas, a United States marshal and his four deputies reined their mounts to a halt and quietly slid from their saddles. After ground-tying the horses, each man pulled a rifle from his saddle boot, and then they hunkered side by side in the dappled shade beneath a stand of cedars, peering at a log cabin nestled some fifty yards deeper in the woods. Disturbed by their presence, birds momentarily flitted about, then realighted in the wind-jostled treetops.

"Okay, men," U.S. Marshal John McCain said, pulling down his Stetson over his wavy black hair, "let's move in real slow. And stay low."

The deputies nodded silently and followed the tall, muscular McCain as he threaded his way through the trees. Stopping about twenty yards from the cabin, McCain dropped to one knee, and the others followed suit. Five horses milled about in a small corral off to one side of the cabin, and a dilapidated old barn stood between the cabin and the corral. After studying the animals for a moment, McCain remarked in a low voice, "Two bays, a black, a big dun, and a piebald—it's them, all right."

One of the deputies looked at the marshal with admiration and said, "You were right, John. Those dirty buzzards doubled back on us."

8

"John's *always* right," declared another. "He's got some kind of sixth sense."

McCain shook his head and explained, "It's just a matter of experience, that's all. These bank robbers seemed to be leaving an awfully clear and obvious trail for us to follow after all the trouble they went through to clean out the Merchants' Bank. I figured that if they were going out of their way to leave such readily perceptible signs, they had something in mind. When the trail suddenly petered out, I guessed that they're expert at covering their tracks and had doubled back for a hideout they had established somewhere near Austin." The lawman tugged on his mustache, and his dark brown eyes reflected his amusement as he added, "It's as simple as that."

One of the younger deputies countered wryly, "Yeah. Simple. Well, I sure hope I'll have developed that kind of 'simple' expertise by the time I've worn a badge as long as you."

"It'll come," replied the thirty-year-old McCain in a fatherly tone.

Looking toward the cabin, John McCain lifted his hat and ran a sleeve across his sweating brow. Then he instructed the others, saying, "The first thing we'll do is sneak in there and take their horses and stash them somewhere back in the woods. Fortunately they can't see the corral because the barn blocks their view, so that should be relatively easy. Once we've done that, we'll surround the place and put those buzzards under arrest." Glancing at each of his men, McCain ordered, "Let's go."

Stealthily, the determined lawmen worked their way through the dense cedars and brush to the corral and then led the outlaws' horses out of sight and left them ground-tied in a gully. That done, the five federal men positioned themselves around the cabin so that every window and both doors were covered. Through the open windows they heard a low rumble of voices, which was punctuated periodically by hoarse laughter.

Marshal John McCain stood behind a tree directly in front of the cabin, rifle ready. He glanced first to his right and then to his left at each of the men flanking the front of the cabin. He was confident that the other deputies were in place and ready at the back of the ramshackle dwelling. Taking a deep breath, McCain peered around the tree and bellowed, "Hey! You in the cabin! You are surrounded by federal officers!"

There was an immediate scraping of chairs and a rumbling of boots on rough wooden flooring. Rapid movement was seen briefly through the windows, but there was no reply.

"I repeat, you are surrounded by federal officers!" shouted McCain. "You are under arrest for bank robbery! Don't try to escape because the doors and windows are all covered! You are to open the front door and throw out all your weapons, then take off your hats and lace your fingers behind your heads and come out slowly . . . one at a time! Now!"

A deep, husky voice hurled a string of profanities at the marshal. Fifteen seconds passed before the front door swung open, showing a shadowed interior—but no one appeared.

"Out with those weapons!" blared McCain.

Finally the same husky voice boomed from inside the dark cabin, "Our guns ain't comin' out, lawman, and neither are we! And you ain't gonna come in after us, either, 'cause we got an ace up our sleeve—and here it is!"

Abruptly a dark-haired girl of about fifteen was pushed into the doorway. Though dressed in dungarees and a man's shirt, she was easily recognizable as a female. Her eyes were bulging in terror, and her voice was fearful as she cried, "Please, Mr. Lawman! Don't let them hurt me! Please!"

One of the deputies near McCain gasped and said, "Where did they get *her*? We can't take them now! She could get hurt—even killed!"

Shaking his head, McCain softly countered, "I think I know who these bandits are." Lifting his voice, he shouted toward the cabin, "Give it up, Hackworth! Throw those guns out like I told you, and come out with your hands on your heads, or we'll blow you out of there with a barrage of hot lead!"

"John!" hissed the deputy in a half whisper. "We can't do it! We might hit the girl!"

"Now, Hackworth!" snarled McCain, disregarding his man's warning.

"Are you blind?" shouted the outlaw. "We got us a hostage, and if you start shootin', I'll blow her head off! Since you know I'm Jed Hackworth, you also know I'm wanted for murder—and you can't hang me twice, lawman! I swear I'll kill the girl unless you get on your horses and hightail it outta here!"

Ignoring the threat, John McCain shouted to his deputies, "Okay, men, listen to me! When I give the signal, start shooting—and don't quit until everybody in the cabin is dead!"

The deputies standing near the marshal stared at him, clearly puzzled. It was obvious that they could not understand why their boss would so willingly jeopardize the girl. McCain had a reputation for ending the careers of outlaws, but never would he sacrifice the life of an innocent child to do so.

"Hackworth!" McCain yelled in his powerful voice. "Are you listening to me? When my men start shooting, bullets will fly through that door and every window! They'll ricochet around inside the cabin like angry hornets, and nobody in there will be safe—including the girl! If you think I'm bluffing, you're about to find out how wrong you can be!"

The girl stood just inside the doorway, wringing her hands, fear etched on her face. There was no word from the cabin.

"Okay, Hackworth!" McCain shouted. "I'm giving you to the count of three! You'd better come out right now, and bring the bank money with you!"

Still no reply and no movement at the door.

"One!" roared McCain.

The deputies glanced at their boss. One of them whispered urgently, "John, be reasonable! I know we've got to obey your orders, but if we have to take part in killing the girl, we're going to have to live with it the rest of our lives!"

McCain merely continued, "Two!"

Suddenly a rifle came sailing out the door past the girl. As it clattered to the ground, it was followed by a Colt .45. "Okay! Okay!" came Hackworth's deep voice. "Don't shoot! We're comin' out!"

The bulky body of Jed Hackworth appeared behind the girl. He had one hand on his head and a canvas money sack in the other. Brushing against the girl, he told her, "Come on. Walk with me."

The deputies sighed with relief as the pair headed toward the tree where U.S. Marshal John McCain waited. Their relief changed to amazement as McCain, holding his rifle on the duo, took them farther back into the woods. There he ordered each of them to stand in front of a slender-trunked tree, and then he handcuffed both the outlaw and the girl to them. McCain then checked to make sure neither one had any concealed weapons.

Returning to his original position, McCain looked toward the cabin and commanded, "The rest of you better follow your boss's example and come out of there immediately!"

His answer was a roar of gunfire.

The lawmen immediately responded. Federal rifles barked repeatedly, shattering glass windows on both sides of the house. The slugs ricocheted and whined angrily within the four walls, and then a howl was heard, followed

JUAREZ **13**

by a thump. Only one outlaw, at the front of the cabin, continued firing.

The lawmen continued their barrage. Suddenly one man dived through a back window and headed for the barn, firing at the deputies stationed at the rear as he ran. Drawing beads on him, the lawmen shot almost simultaneously, and the outlaw fell to the ground, his revolver flying from his hand. Still alive, he crawled toward the gun with blood pumping from his bullet wounds and, gritting his teeth, he grasped the weapon and brought it up to fire again at the lawmen.

The deputies shot him again. This time he went down for good.

The remaining outlaw in the cabin suddenly ceased firing. Figuring the man had stopped to reload his gun, John McCain raced toward the cabin, drawing his revolver. "Cover me!" he shouted at his men.

Instantly obeying, the deputies unleashed a hail of lead on the windows.

When McCain bolted through the door, he found the outlaw on his knees, snapping the cylinder of his gun into place. "Drop it!" the marshal commanded, leveling his weapon on him.

The man had a wild look in his eyes, and it was clear that at that moment the word "surrender" was not in his vocabulary. Roaring like some wild animal, the outlaw brought the weapon to bear.

McCain pulled the trigger of his gun, and it bucked against his palm. A black hole appeared in the man's forehead, and the impact of the slug flopped him onto his back. His right foot twitched for a few seconds and then went still.

Glancing quickly at the other outlaw, who lay on the floor next to an overturned table, McCain saw there was a jagged hole in his temple where a bullet had caught him. Relieved that the siege was over with none of his men hurt, the marshal started outside.

The other lawmen were closing in on the cabin as John McCain appeared at the door, punching the spent shell from his gun and slipping in a live cartridge. "Only dead ones in here," he said advisedly as his men drew up.

"We got the one who came out the window, John," one of his deputies informed him.

"Good," the marshal said as he slipped his revolver back in its holster. "You gentlemen do nice work."

"You're not so bad yourself," quipped one of the deputies. "But, John, you've got to tell us why that girl is handcuffed to a tree out there with that killer."

Before McCain could reply, another deputy asked, "And were you really going to start shooting with that girl standing there?"

"I knew we wouldn't have to," McCain answered, grinning. "You see, boys, what we've got handcuffed to those trees over there are *two* killers. She's Jed Hackworth's daughter. Myrna Hackworth is only fifteen years old, but she's already killed three men that I know of . . . all in cold blood. She's been traveling with her father since she was ten or eleven. As soon as I saw Myrna, I knew Jed would be in there—and I also knew he wasn't about to let his daughter be killed. The hostage bit, as you can see, was only a ruse."

"Whew!" gasped the deputy. "For a minute there, we all thought you'd lost your mind!"

McCain lifted his hat, ran his fingers through his dark, wavy hair, and chuckled. "What's the matter with you boys? Don't you have any faith in me?"

"I just about lost it," the young deputy admitted. "But now I don't think I'll ever doubt you again."

McCain laughed and then countered, "What do you want to bet? Chances are pretty good I'll scare all of you again sometime." Then, gesturing with his thumb over his shoulder, he told the men, "Time to head for town. Let's gather up these bodies and our prisoners."

*   *   *

Howard Wheeler, chief United States marshal of the Austin office, was sitting at his desk, rubbing the gray fringe on the back of his nearly bald head in consternation. Sighing, he glanced out the window beside his desk just as John McCain and his deputies rode into town. Startled, he stood and stepped close to the window to get a better look, and a broad smile broke over his weathered face as he beheld the procession.

At that moment, Deputy Marshal Joe Biggs came through Wheeler's open office door and said excitedly, "Boss, John McCain's back and—Oh, I guess you can see that."

"Sure can," Wheeler rejoined. "And I'm glad to see that at least there are three outlaws who'll never rob another bank." He paused and then asked, "Know who the big man and the girl are?"

"No, sir."

"Jed Hackworth and his female brat."

"Jed Hackworth!" exclaimed Biggs, surprised. "Some catch for John, huh?"

"What's new?" Wheeler responded wryly, still watching the slow-moving procession.

Just then John McCain looked toward the office and waved to his boss. Wheeler gave him a big smile and waved back.

When they passed from view, the chief U.S. marshal sat down behind his desk and said, "Joe, if you and your fellow deputies develop into just *half* of what John McCain is, we'll have us an unbeatable team here in Austin." Sticking a dead, half-smoked cigar in his mouth, Wheeler added, "I wish I had a dozen like him." Narrowing his eyes, he corrected himself, "Make that *two* dozen!"

The young deputy shook his head. "The man's a marvel, Chief. I don't think he knows what fear is."

"Sure he does," countered Wheeler, biting down on the dead cigar. "He fears *failure*. There isn't an ounce of quit in him. He's your example, Joe. Study the man carefully."

"I will, sir," Biggs murmured and then returned to the outer office where he had been doing his paperwork.

Nearly a half hour had passed when Chief Howard Wheeler heard voices in the outer office and recognized them as those of John McCain and the men who had gone with him to chase down the bank robbers. Removing the lifeless cigar still clamped between his teeth, he looked up to see the tall, broad-shouldered figure of his favorite marshal filling the doorway.

McCain thumbed his hat to the back of his head, adjusted his low-slung gun belt, and asked, "I guess you know who I found?"

"Yeah. Jed Hackworth."

"Right. The sheriff's got him and his daughter locked up tight. The undertaker's got the other three, and the bank has its money back in the vault."

"Good job!" exclaimed Wheeler. "Sit down and tell me how you caught them."

McCain took ten minutes to tell the story. When he had finished, the chief said, "You're a good man, John. You did well. I wish I had more like you."

"Hey, boss," McCain responded, leaning forward in his chair, "don't forget, I didn't do it by myself! Moffitt, Mentor, Carter, and Nelson were there, too."

With a dismissive wave of his hand, Wheeler said, "I wouldn't rob them of their due credit for a minute, but you and I both know they would never have done it by themselves."

"They're coming along, Chief. It won't be long till they'll be able to take on these outlaw-chasing jobs without a nursemaid."

"Well, they're going to have to learn plenty fast, because you won't be around for a spell. I've got a new assignment for you, my friend . . . one that only *you* can pull off."

McCain leaned back in his chair, studying Wheeler's face. Chuckling, he quipped, "Why is it I always get this buttering-up business before I get a dirty job?"

Wheeler cocked his head, frowned, and gestured with the cigar stub. "What do you mean, 'buttering-up business'? This isn't buttering you up, my boy. You know the confidence I have in you. Now, are you ready to listen to the details of your assignment?"

Rubbing his thick mustache, McCain grinned crookedly and nodded. "Sure, boss. Shoot."

"We've got a serious situation down in Mexico," began the chief United States marshal. "Three weeks ago, a group of Guatemalan men stirred up trouble at a political meeting down in New Orleans, and when law officers tried to quell the disturbance, a gunfight broke out. Two officers were wounded, but far worse, a Guatemalan bullet struck Louisiana's governor, killing him."

McCain's face grew immediately sober. "Oh, no! I hadn't heard about it, Chief. I don't think I've had time to read a newspaper for over a month. Go on."

"The Guatemalans are now being held in a New Orleans jail, awaiting trial. But there's a touchy element here. One of the men is the son of Guatemala's *presidente*, Enrique Cresada."

The younger marshal nodded. "A most delicate and sticky situation."

Wheeler proceeded, "Several days ago a series of important meetings was held down in Juárez between the U.S. secretary of war, Duncan Campbell, and Mexico's Generalissimo Fernando Velásquez. The talks were intended to resolve tensions following that Mexican uprising near San Antonio. You know the one."

"Oh, yeah. When that group took over the Alamo, saying they were claiming it once again for Mexico."

"Right. And you'll remember that several people were injured in the fight that took place when those Texas patriots charged in and pitched the Mexicans out."

"The Mexicans got the worst of it, as I recall. Didn't the patriots beat them up pretty bad, then drag them all the way to the border and throw them rather roughly back into their own country?"

"They did, indeed. As a matter of fact, a couple of the Mexicans were crippled for life. Anyway, on the evening of the last day of meetings, a band of Guatemalan guerrillas kidnapped Duncan Campbell and his family from the hotel where they were staying in Juárez."

"His family?" McCain asked in surprise. "He had his family with him?"

"Yes. His wife and twenty-two-year-old daughter. But it's worse than just a kidnapping. Some American friends of the Campbells were with them in their hotel suite when the Guatemalans forced their way in—the Stanford family of El Paso. The guerrillas knifed them to death—the man, his wife, and their teenage son."

McCain's mouth hardened. Then he asked, "So where did the Guatemalans take the Campbells?"

"You know where Chihuahua is?"

"Yeah. A few hundred miles south of Juárez."

"Two hundred and thirty-five to be exact. Well, the guerrillas are holding them in a secluded, well-fortified mansion a few miles outside Chihuahua. I understand the place is a virtual fort. Of course they've tried to keep their hideout a secret."

"How'd you find out where they are holding them?"

"Several Mexican men just happened to see from a distance what was going on when the Campbells were first moved into the mansion. They reported it to the authorities, who in turn reported it to our office in El Paso. I believe you know Chief Marshal Eldridge Harris down there, don't you?"

"Yes."

"Harris and I have kept the wires hot all afternoon. He says the Guatemalans are using Mexicans as mediators to make known their demands."

"It isn't hard to guess what they want. All of their boys set free, right?"

"Exactly," agreed the chief, vigorously nodding his bald head. "They've telegraphed their terms to New Orleans from Chihuahua, via Juárez and El Paso—thinking they could keep their location a secret—instructing that their countrymen be freed by May nineteenth, or the Campbells will be executed."

John McCain took off his hat and laid it on the corner of Wheeler's desk. "What's the Mexican government doing about the situation?"

"Not a thing," Wheeler answered dryly. "The Mexicans are remaining neutral. After all, they *are* bordered on the southeast by Guatemala. They believe if they interfere, it would damage relations between themselves and their southern neighbors."

McCain's face reddened with anger. "Well, how about the relationship with their *northern* neighbors? Aren't they concerned about that? After all, isn't that what Campbell and Velásquez's meetings were all about?"

"Sure were," replied Wheeler. "I'm certain they're concerned about their relationship with us, but they're at least equally concerned about the Guatemalans. One thing I have to say for them—when their authorities received word as to the whereabouts of the Campbells, they immediately informed us."

"I appreciate that," McCain responded, his voice ironic. "So what's the attitude of the authorities in New Orleans?"

"Just what it ought to be. The state of Louisiana and the federal government are refusing to release the Guatemalans, saying that to do so would encourage similar acts of violence in the future."

McCain shifted on the chair. "They're dead right about that."

"This incident has the attention of the President himself, needless to say."

"That's understandable," said McCain. "Duncan Campbell is a mighty important man."

Wheeler picked up a telegram on the desk and held it in his hand. "This came less than an hour ago . . . straight from Grover Cleveland. He's ordered a special rescue mission to free the Campbells from Guatemalan hands, and he asked me to put my best man on it—and *you* are that man, John." Wheeler paused a few seconds and stared intently at his underling. Then he said, "But because of the obvious and extreme danger involved, I won't make it an order."

Before McCain could respond, the chief went on. "I should tell you this: There have been other problems with Guatemalans in Mexico for the past year or more. I don't know the reasons, but the Guatemalan guerrillas have a network of men hiding out all over Mexico, headed by a clever and resourceful cutthroat named José Gristo. And when I say cutthroat, I mean it. Word is that Gristo personally led the abduction of the Campbells and that the Stanford family died mercilessly and brutally on his orders. From what I'm told, the guerrillas are smart and plenty tough. If you go after them, my friend, you'll be taking a genuine risk with your life. One tiny slipup, and you and the Campbells will be dead." Looking his favorite marshal squarely in the eye, Wheeler asked, "Are you getting the picture?"

"Quite clearly," the handsome lawman assured his boss.

"If you take the assignment, the plans you devise for the rescue will have to be kept as secret as possible. There may well be Mexicans who are sympathetic to the cause of the Guatemalan guerrillas . . . whatever that is."

"I assume you've got somebody down there ready to help me."

"You bet. Luckily Eldridge Harris knows of some Mexicans who are very much opposed to the guerrillas and their activities and who are also friends of the United States. He says they can be trusted completely—and they're eager to help in the rescue."

"I'll say one thing for you, Chief," McCain remarked. "You do a good job laying groundwork."

"That's my small part of the rescue operation, John. The big part will be yours. How about it? Will you take the job?"

McCain flashed his crooked grin and stood, taking his hat from the desk. Wheeler rose with him, waiting for the man's reply . . . as if he did not already know what it would be.

Dropping the Stetson on his head, the muscular McCain said, "Sounds like a real challenge, boss—and you know me. I've never been able to ignore a challenge."

"Yeah," Wheeler said, the satisfaction he was feeling written all over his face. "I know."

"I suppose you also know when the next train leaves Austin for El Paso."

"It just so happens I do," the chief admitted, chuckling. "It's scheduled to pull out tomorrow evening at six-ten. You can get a good night's sleep on the way, and you'll arrive in El Paso at nine-fifteen the following morning."

"A good night's sleep, huh?" snickered McCain. "You ever try to sleep sitting up on one of those hard coach seats?"

"You won't be sitting up, my friend," replied Wheeler. "I've already reserved a Pullman for you. Private compartment. Your own bed."

"Already put my name on it, eh?"

"Already," came the quick answer. There was a twinkle in Wheeler's eye.

"Pretty sure of yourself, aren't you?"

"Yep. Like you said a moment ago, I know you. You're that badge-toting son-of-a-gun who can't ignore a challenge!"

"You also know I speak Spanish. Who would you have sent if I didn't?"

"You."

"Even if I didn't know a word of Spanish?"

"Sure. You'd just have to stay awake all night on the train and read a Spanish dictionary."

McCain laughed and headed for the door. "I'll see you in the morning, Chief."

"Okay. Meanwhile I'll wire Harris and tell him to meet you at the depot in El Paso."

Chapter Two

At just after nine o'clock on the morning of May 9, 1893, U.S. Marshal John McCain watched out the window of his Pullman compartment as the train began to slow down. The morning sun was casting its glow on the rugged, barren Franklin Mountains to the west of the tough border town of El Paso. To the north were the sunbleached badlands of New Mexico, while to the south was Old Mexico, her hazy purple mountains outlined against the clear sky. The natural border separating the two countries was the Rio Grande, winding lazily and sinuously southward, and just across the river lay Ciudad Juárez.

The big locomotive chugged into the El Paso station and hissed to a stop. Standing, McCain put on his hat, grasped his small suitcase and then left the compartment and hurried toward the rear door. When he stepped outside onto the small platform, he scanned the crowd of people waiting for the train's arrival, quickly finding the tall, slender man who had come to meet him. It was easy to spot Chief U.S. Marshal Eldridge Harris, for even with a wide-brimmed hat on, his carrot-red hair was readily visible, along with the bushy mustache of the same color.

Smiling, Harris approached the train, weaving through the crowd. As the younger lawman stepped onto the depot platform, Harris drew up to McCain and exclaimed, "John! It's been a long time. How are you?"

"Fine, sir," replied McCain. "And you?"

As they shook hands, Harris replied, "The same. My, it is good to see you! I've heard glowing reports about your work these past few years."

Chuckling, McCain said, "Don't believe everything Chief Wheeler tells you, sir. He gives a lot of credit to me when it should go to the men who work with me."

"Same old John, I see," murmured Harris. "Never been one for the limelight, have you?"

"I just do my job, Chief," McCain said quietly. "And speaking of which, let's talk about the one I'm about to tackle."

The two federal lawmen left the depot and headed down the street toward Harris's office. As they walked, Harris described the network that the brutal Guatemalan guerrillas had established throughout Mexico, adding that the rescue would have to involve as few people as possible in order to keep it from being exposed.

They reached the office and went inside, and McCain was introduced to two deputy marshals who were sitting on the corners of their desks, cleaning their guns. Going into the chief's private office, McCain and Harris sat facing each other across the chief's desk. Without preamble, the redheaded man said, "John, I've got two trusted friends in Chihuahua. One is Rondo Ortega, and the other is Ray Gonzales. Ortega has a carpentry business there, and Gonzales leads a tough band of fighters who were active against insurgents in the Mexican revolution two years ago. Gonzales and his men now live in the hills near town, where they're still cleaning up the troublemakers who fomented the revolution."

"Sounds like a pretty rough bunch."

Harris smiled. "Ray Gonzales is so tough, I wouldn't be surprised if he eats nails for breakfast."

"Sounds like just the kind of man I want on my side," McCain remarked with a sly grin. "Now, just exactly what are Ortega and Gonzales going to do to help me?"

"They're both prepared to provide you with manpower, horses, weapons, and anything else needed to carry out the rescue."

"How many men does Gonzales have?"

"I'm not sure, but if he doesn't have as many as you think you'll need, he's got plenty of contacts. He can probably raise you an army if you want one—although, as I said, it might be wiser to keep the numbers as low as possible."

"Well, I won't know for sure what I'll need till I get there and take a look at the situation, but I'm sure I'll need quite a few men. As long as they're trustworthy, the numbers shouldn't pose any problem." McCain was quiet for a few seconds and then said, "As I see it, I've got two basic dilemmas to solve. The first is how to get the Campbells out of the place where they're being held, and the second is how to get them safely back here to El Paso." He sighed, muttering, "There's a lot of real estate between Chihuahua and the Rio Grande."

"Well, as for problem number one," Harris mused, "I can't help you. There's no way to make plans about that until you've seen the layout. But I've already been working on problem number two."

"Oh?"

"Yep. Through Rondo Ortega, I've arranged for the Campbells to be transported by stagecoach from Chihuahua to Juárez."

"Stagecoach?" McCain's brow furrowed. "Won't that leave the secretary and his family vulnerable to being captured again?"

"I'm open to a better suggestion," replied Harris, "but hear me out first, okay?"

"Sure," McCain agreed, rocking the straight-backed chair onto its back legs and folding his arms across his muscular chest. "I'm all ears."

"All right. Let's think like the Guatemalans for a moment. If you were a guerrilla leader and you found out that someone had broken into the place where the Campbells were being held and had freed them, where would you figure the rescuers would take them?"

"Back to the states, of course. Texas."

"Right. And by what means of transportation?"

McCain thought a moment and then replied, "Horseback. That would be the fastest."

Harris smiled. "Go to the head of the class, my boy. That's exactly as the guerrilla leader would think. Okay, so you've put the Campbells on horses. What route would you take from Chihuahua to the Texas border?"

The answer came quickly. "Well, I'd definitely stay off the roads to avoid being seen. And we'd ride through the back country, taking the shortest, most direct possible route."

"Congratulations again, Marshal McCain. So if you were a Guatemalan guerrilla leader and you wanted to recapture the Campbells, you would send your troops in swarms throughout the back country, looking for a group of riders. Correct?"

The picture suddenly became clear to John McCain. "Ah, so that's it! Outsmart the guerrillas by doing the unexpected and putting the Campbells on a stagecoach— which the guerrillas are accustomed to seeing on the roads. Pretty smart, sir. I think you've got something there."

"If you can come up with a better idea, I'm ready to listen," said Harris.

Shaking his head, McCain remarked, "I don't think there *is* a better idea, Chief. Now, correct me if I'm wrong, but you'd just put the Campbells on a regularly scheduled stagecoach?"

"That's right. The guerrillas would be watching the back country like hawks. A stagecoach on a regular run would be quite inconspicuous."

After thinking silently a moment, McCain peered at the chief and then suggested, "Maybe we should let the first scheduled stagecoach after the rescue is accomplished de-

part without the Campbells. I mean, just in case the idea
of a coach being used should occur to one of the guerrillas.
If they stopped it and didn't find the Campbells, they'd
probably figure they'd been mistaken in thinking a stagecoach would be used to transport the Campbells out of the
country."

"Keep them hidden somewhere and put them on the
next scheduled coach, eh?" Harris said, rubbing his chin.
"That's good thinking, John."

"Then, of course, the coach that actually carries the
Campbells would be manned by myself and some of Gonzales's men . . . all of us armed to the teeth."

"Of course," agreed Harris.

"So, how did we come by having a stagecoach avail-
able?" queried McCain.

"Well, it just so happens that the head agent of the
Alegre Viaje Stage Line in Chihuahua is a very close
friend of Rondo Ortega's. His name's Julio Herrera. Herrera has promised to help in every way he can, and Rondo
says the man is absolutely trustworthy."

"Good!" declared John McCain, slapping his thighs with
his palms and then getting to his feet. "I think we've got
the second part of the operation worked out—now I've got
to concentrate on the first part. You say Gonzales and his
bunch are tough?"

"Tough as pig iron, son," the chief promised, grinning.
Also rising, he added, "I guarantee you, they can match
any Guatemalan guerrillas—and then some."

It was high noon in the city of Chihuahua, Mexico, on
May 13, 1893, when Rondo Ortega pulled his wagon to a
halt across the street from the Alegre Viaje Stage Line
office. Noting that the coach from Juárez had not yet
arrived, he was hardly surprised. It seldom arrived on
time. Both horses snorted as he wrapped the reins around
the brake handle and alighted from the wagon.

A short and very slender man—who like many of his

fellow countrymen wore long sideburns and a bushy mustache—Rondo Ortega was a widower in his early forties whose wife had died of fever some five years previously. He lived alone on a small place about a mile south of town, where he maintained his carpentry shop and raised a few head of cattle, along with some pigs and chickens. Ortega was also a patriot, and he intensely disliked revolutionaries . . . especially those from other countries who used his country and his people to their own ends.

Leaning against the wagon, Ortega gazed northward beyond the flat-roofed adobe buildings that lined Chihuahua's main street. The street was active with buggies, wagons, carts, riders, and pedestrians. Movement caught Ortega's eye at the stage line office across the street and he glanced over to see Rubin Lupino, Julio Herrera's young assistant, come outside and also look northward. Then, carefully threading his way between vehicles rolling in both directions, Ortega crossed the dusty street and said, *"Buenos días,* Rubin. You are looking for the stagecoach also, eh?"

"Sí," Lupino answered, smiling. "It should be arriving very soon. You are here to meet the *gringo* lawman, no?"

Ortega looked at the young man sharply. "How do you know about this man?"

"Julio Herrera told me."

Rondo Ortega nodded slowly. His good friend had felt it safe to confide in his young assistant, and he had faith in Herrera's judgment. Finally answering Lupino's question, Ortega said, *"Sí.* I was hoping it would not be late for a change, but—"

Ortega's words were cut off by a shout from up the street and the sudden sound of rumbling hooves, and he turned and saw the stagecoach coming. The vehicle was an Abbott-Downing Concord coach that had been purchased from one of the stage lines in the United States that had been forced out of business by the railroads. Rubin Lupino had repainted the coach and redone the lettering on the panel that ran below the luggage rack to read: Alegre Viaje Stage Line. Though it was covered with dust, it was still an object of beauty as it bobbed serenely down the street behind the prancing six-up team with chains jangling and harness rings shining in the noonday sun.

The coach halted in a cloud of dust. Rubin Lupino greeted the two men up in the box and then stepped beside the vehicle and opened the door. Rondo Ortega drew near, eager to see the face of the United States marshal. He did not have to wait long, for the first person to alight was tall, handsome John McCain, who then turned to help two Mexican ladies from the coach.

Though there was no badge on the chest of the broad-shouldered American, Ortega was sure this was the marshal. Walking up to him, he asked quietly in accented English, "You are Marshal McCain, *señor?*"

McCain's white teeth shone in contrast to his suntanned skin as he smiled and replied, "*Sí, Señor . . . ah . . . Ortega?*"

The two men shook hands, chatting briefly, and Ortega was amazed at how well the *gringo* lawman spoke Spanish. After a few minutes, however, they agreed to speak to each other in English.

Interrupting Rubin Lupino from his chore of unloading the luggage, Ortega asked if Julio Herrera was in the office, wanting him to meet McCain as well. But Lupino told him that Herrera was out of town and would not return until evening.

Ortega turned to the marshal, who was now holding his small satchel, and suggested, "You can meet Julio later, Marshal. Right now, I will take you to my home so you can relax, and then we will talk of your purpose for being here."

The Mexican led McCain across the street, and as they climbed into Ortega's wagon, he remarked, "Marshal McCain, am I to presume that you are not wearing a badge to keep your identity hidden?"

"You're right, Señor Ortega," McCain replied. "I took it off before I crossed the border at Juárez. Since, as you know, my mission here is to be as secret as possible, I didn't think I should alert people that I am a lawman." He suddenly grinned, adding, "So to that end, why don't you call me John?"

Ortega chuckled. "Of course. And you must call me Rondo."

The ride to Rondo Ortega's place was not far, and when they turned off the road and pulled into the yard, Ortega hauled the wagon to a stop near the door of his large stone barn, the roof of which was made of sod. As they stepped down from the wagon, the smaller man said, "When Chief Harris informed me of this secret undertaking, I decided that I am going to keep you in a very special place. Come, let me show you."

Rondo Ortega led John McCain into the interior of the stone structure and closed the big door behind them, thrusting them into near darkness, as the only light came from a series of small windows in the walls some eight feet above the dirt floor. McCain stayed on Ortega's heels as the Mexican moved to a far corner of the barn where a feed barrel stood next to a long wooden trough that paralleled one wall. Ortega suddenly grasped the barrel and turned it onto its side, exposing the square wooden trapdoor that the bottom of the barrel was attached to. The opening led into a cellar beneath the barn floor.

"You should wait here, John," Ortega suggested as he began to descend on a ladder. "Let me light a lantern first."

Moments later, yellow light illuminated the black shaft, and the Mexican stood ten feet below. "You may come down now," Ortega said, gesturing with the lantern in his hand.

McCain's eyes widened when he reached the bottom and found himself standing in complete living quarters. Ortega quickly lit four more lanterns that hung on nails,

one on each wall, illuminating the entire room. The secret
cellar was some thirty by forty feet in size and was equipped
with four cots for sleeping, as well as with a table and
several chairs. There was also food stocked on shelves,
along with canvas water bags—and an arsenal of rifles and
handguns and plenty of ammunition.

Before the marshal could comment, Ortega smiled at
him and remarked, "I see that you are somewhat amazed
by this, but I can easily explain it. At the time of the
revolution two years ago, I equipped this cellar with these
living quarters and the firearms you see before you. I
planned to use it as a hiding place if the revolutionaries
were successful in overthrowing the Mexican government.
Thank the dear Lord in heaven that did not happen—
however, now it will make an excellent hiding place for
you in case the Guatemalans should somehow learn of
your presence and why you are here."

Thumbing his hat to the back of his head, the lawman
shook his head in wonderment and commented, "Mighty
nice headquarters, I'd say, Rondo. Why, you've even laid
a wooden floor *and* covered it with carpet."

"Nothing but the best," the Mexican responded with a
grin. "You will see that I have also built wooden walls and
covered them with adobe. This is to keep the dampness out."

"Well, it works, my good friend," McCain said with
admiration. "You'd never know it was a cellar by the feel
of it. I will be very comfortable down here."

"You will also be very safe," added Rondo.

Noticing two solid doors in one wall, the marshal asked,
"What's behind those doors?"

"Those are storerooms," answered the little Mexican.
"Not much in them at the moment." He looked around
and then asked, "Now that we have you situated, where
do you wish to begin?"

McCain explained, "The first thing I want to do is take a
look at the place where the guerrillas have the Campbell
family incarcerated."

Nodding, Ortega said, "Of course. However, it might be best that we wait until the sun has gone down. The place is surrounded on three sides by dense forest, but it is some distance from the trees to the mansion. You will need to observe it from the edge of the trees, and it would be safer if we wait until the light is dim."

"All right," agreed McCain. "I'm sure you know best about that. Do you have a pair of binoculars?"

"Sí," Ortega replied. "I have them in the house." He grinned, adding, "And of course I will lend you a horse and not make you walk."

McCain laughed. "Excellent. Tell me a little about this mansion. It is an actual mansion?"

"It is. The place was owned by a very wealthy cattle baron many years ago, and as I remember, there are twelve bedrooms in it. It is built with thick adobe walls, and there is an exterior wall about five feet high all the way around the mansion. It is almost literally a fort—and it will not be easy to get inside."

"I figured on that," responded McCain. "What kind of a gate do they have?"

"It is of wrought iron, and it is the same height as the wall. The bars on the gate are only about ten inches apart—too narrow to squeeze through."

"I see. Am I correct in assuming that it is a two-story building?"

"Sí."

"Okay, partner," the marshal said with a smile. "You've helped me to know a little bit of what I'm up against. Now I'm looking forward to seeing the place for myself. Incidentally, when will I meet Ray Gonzales?"

"It will probably be the day after tomorrow. That is as soon as I could get Ray to put aside what he is doing and come. He could show up tomorrow, but I doubt it." Ortega gestured at one of the cots and suggested, "Perhaps you wish to rest for a while after your long journey. It is still many hours until darkness."

McCain grinned. "You don't have to offer twice, my friend."

As the sun slipped behind the mountains to the west, U.S. Marshal John McCain and Rondo Ortega guided their mounts through the dense, hilly forest just north of the huge adobe mansion where Duncan Campbell and his family were being held hostage. The two men dismounted on a commanding height about a quarter mile from the mansion, and leaving the horses tied deep in the forest, they crept to the edge of the trees. As the mansion and its outbuildings came into view, the marshal whistled softly, saying, "That *is* some fortress, all right."

"You have a big job cut out for you," Ortega mused, shaking his head.

John McCain peered through the binoculars and studied the layout of the place. The mansion faced eastward, toward a dusty road that ran north and south about forty yards from the front wall. The road in turn was a short distance from the edge of the forest. On the south side of the mansion lay a broad, sweeping valley of lush green pastures, bisected by a creek that snaked across it.

After several minutes, McCain announced, "I need to get a better look. You stay here while I circle around and view it from different angles."

The tall lawman worked his way in a circle eastward, staying just inside the perimeter of the trees, and when he reached the front of the mansion, he hunkered down in some bushes. He could clearly see the heads of the guards pacing continuously behind the five-foot-high adobe wall—a couple on the east, another pair on the south, and two more on the north. He assumed there would be a fourth pair at the back of the house on the west side as well.

McCain's spine tingled slightly when two of the patrolling guards met each other behind the large wrought iron gate, for he saw that the guards had large male dogs at their heels. The lawman recognized the dogs as Doberman pinschers, a breed that had been developed in Germany within the past few years. Dobermans were known to be fast, intelligent, and easily trained to be vicious. Wondering if all the guards were equally supplied, the marshal reasoned he had to figure eight dogs into his calculations of obstacles that needed surmounting.

Noting that the sky was growing dimmer, John McCain hurried through the woods, past Rondo Ortega, and made his way to the back side of the mansion. McCain found that there were indeed two guards at that end. Wanting to see as much as he could, he climbed a huge tree until he was some thirty feet off the ground. His suspicions were confirmed: The guards on the back side also had Dobermans.

Abruptly, movement on the flat roof of the mansion caught his eye. A three-foot-high wall ran around the perimeter of the roof, and there was a rifleman occupying each side. Obviously the Guatemalans were taking no chances. McCain told himself it would be next to impossible to shoot those men on the roof from the ground.

From his high perch, McCain watched two guards come around the corner of the building and then take the places of the guards who had been on duty. It was evident that there was a changing of the guard just before dark.

Now that he had learned the setup at the mansion, McCain began descending the tree. Pondering the situation, he knew he must find a way to eliminate the dogs and the guards, while at the same time preventing the guerrillas inside the mansion from killing the Campbells when the attack was launched.

McCain was just about to swing from a low limb and drop to the ground when a cold voice from the base of the tree snapped, "Hold it, *gringo*! Stop where you are!"

Gripping the limb, McCain looked down in the dwindling light and saw two vicious-looking Guatemalan guerrillas staring up at him, their revolvers pointed at his chest.

The same man then commanded, "Now, reach very

carefully for your revolver and lift it out of the holster with the tips of your fingers. Then drop it to me gently."

McCain's gaze briefly shifted to the two ominous black bores that were lined on him before looking back into the fierce eyes of the guerrillas. While easing the gun from its holster, McCain realized that unless he could kill the men then and there, the entire rescue scheme would be washed up. And he had to do it without a shot being fired, for the sound would bring the Guatemalans swarming from the mansion. His mind was working fast as he let the Colt .45 slip from his fingers and drop into the waiting hand of the man who had done the speaking.

The Guatemalan commanded, "Climb down now, *gringo*. Very slowly."

Every muscle in John McCain's body was wire-tight. What he was going to do would take precision timing and absolute accuracy. Both men were standing quite close to the muscular lawman as his feet touched the ground. With the quickness of a panther, McCain unleashed a sledge-hammer blow to the jaw of the man who had his gun, and the guerrilla went down, unconscious. Following through with the same smooth move that had dropped the first guerrilla, the marshal sent a violent kick to the groin of the second one, doubling him over in agony.

Quickly McCain grabbed the man and clamped a hand over his mouth. The guerrilla struggled valiantly, but his strength could not match that of John McCain's, and the marshal rammed his head against the tree with terrific force, cracking the man's skull. The Guatemalan went limp and fell to the ground, dead.

The other man was stirring and beginning to come around, and the lawman stepped behind him and hoisted him to a sitting position. Dropping to one knee, he locked the man's head in the crook of his left arm and gripped the guerrilla's chin with his right hand. McCain then gave it a sharp jerk sideways, snapping the man's neck. The guerrilla's body went limp like a rag doll and the marshal let him fall. He sent a quick glance toward the mansion. No one appeared.

Holstering his gun, McCain jammed the other two revolvers under his belt and dragged the bodies away by the shirt collars. He took them deep into the timber, hiding them temporarily in a thick clump of bushes and then hurried through the almost total darkness to where he had left Rondo Ortega.

"Rondo!" he called softly. "Are you there?"

"*Sí*, John!" came the immediate reply from the deep shadows. "What took so long? I was afraid something happened to you, and I was not sure what to do."

McCain quickly informed Ortega of the attack. Then he said, "I think it would be best to take the bodies somewhere and dispose of them so the other guerrillas won't find them. It'd be better that they wonder what became of them than to know they had been killed."

"That is good thinking," replied Ortega. "There is a dense thicket at my place where we can bury them, and no one will ever find them."

Groping their way through the forest in the deep gloom that surrounded them, they found the bodies and dragged them to the horses. Draping the corpses on one horse, Ortega and McCain rode double on the other. As they headed for the Mexican's farm, McCain told him about the Doberman pinschers being used by the guerrillas, and they thought about their next course of action.

Inside the guerrilla stronghold, the Campbells were trying to make the best of their dire situation. By the light of the one lamp they had been allowed, they were eating a meal of beans and hardtack in the large bedroom where they were kept locked up. They could hear guards pacing the hallway and, being on the ground floor, they could also distinctly hear the movements of the guards and dogs outside on the grounds.

Upon learning of the demands of the guerrillas, the

Campbells were horrified that they were being used as pawns to such an end. Knowing they could do nothing to alter their situation, beyond enduring it stoically, they prayed for rescue—although given the seeming imperviousness of the stronghold, deliverance seemed unlikely. They could only hope they would be released, for the war secretary knew that the President would never give in to the guerrillas' demand that they be exchanged for the Guatemalans.

Patricia Campbell was having the most difficulty in maintaining her composure, fearing not for herself, but for her husband and her daughter. She slept fitfully, awakening many times during the long nights, her sleep haunted by nightmares. Lucy found herself thrust into the role of comforter, fearing that even if by some slim chance they were rescued, the ordeal might take permanent toll on her mother. Duncan Campbell had at first raised the specter of retaliation and had tried using intimidation against the Guatemalans. But realizing his threats against the outlaws were futile, Campbell gave them up, and now he dozed for long stretches at a time.

None of the Campbells had much appetite, but they consumed what food was given them in order to keep up their strength. As they washed down the last few beans with thick, bitter coffee, Lucy looked across the small table that had been provided for them and said, "Father, when we first arrived here and were told the situation, you said someone would come to our rescue—but obviously nothing has happened. What do you think now?"

Trying to remain calm and keep an air of optimism before his wife and daughter, Duncan Campbell replied, "There are still several days left, honey. And while President Cleveland certainly will not give in to the guerrillas' demands, he won't ignore our plight. I'm sure of it."

Patricia's face was drawn and ashen. "Duncan," she said shakily, "you've explained it to us before, but I just don't understand. Why doesn't the government simply release those Guatemalans from jail? Would our country let us die just for the sake of punishing a few foreigners? What about us? Don't we count?"

"Of course we do, dear," Campbell responded, trying to smile. "But as I told you, to release the prisoners would encourage other people in the world also to do violent things. It wouldn't be long before anarchists could get away with anything they so desired. I'm quite sure the Guatemalan prisoners will not be released. The only thing we can hope for is rescue by our own countrymen."

There was despair in Patricia's voice as she murmured, "We're a long way from Juárez. Even if our countrymen wanted to rescue us, how would they know where to look?"

"It no doubt would take a little time, but it could be done."

"Time is something we have very little of, Duncan," Patricia rejoined bitterly. "What's tearing my heart out is Lucy having to die before she's barely had the chance to live."

Patricia abruptly broke into sobs and leapt to her feet, hurrying to a corner of the room. Duncan and Lucy followed, embracing the despairing woman. When Patricia's weeping subsided, the secretary told her softly, "We've still got five days. Let's keep our chins up and pray God will speed rescuers to us. They just have to be coming. They just have to."

Chapter Three

Lucy Campbell lay awake in the dark room, unable to sleep. She had decided that perhaps they should no longer wait for a rescue attempt that might not come. Maybe they should try to initiate their own escape.

But how? All the guerrillas were armed with revolvers, rifles, and knives, not to mention the vicious dogs. What could the Campbells do against them? Escape was virtually impossible, unless . . .

Earlier that day, Lucy had examined their quarters very carefully, including the spacious walk-in closet in the bedroom where they were imprisoned. She had noticed a spike protruding from a closet wall, and she figured the point had to be sharp. Maybe it could serve as a weapon just long enough for her to get hold of a gun. The chance for success was slim, but it was better than quietly waiting to be executed.

Slipping from her bed, Lucy put on the robe she had been provided with and, by the light of the moon coming through the bedroom windows, made her way to the closet. The door creaked slightly as she pulled it open, and she moved it slowly to keep the sound to a minimum. Once inside, she felt her way along the wall until her hand touched the spike. As she worked it in a circular fashion, she was pleased to find that it was not buried deeply in the wall. Within seconds, it was loose and in her hand.

39

Emerging from the closet and gliding softly across the room, Lucy looked at the lamplight seeping under the door. Every night so far there had been only one guard sitting in the hall. She hoped nothing had changed.

After making sure her parents were still asleep, and with the spike in her right hand tucked into the sleeve of her robe, the lovely blonde tapped lightly on the door, her heart pounding as she waited for the guard to respond. If the Guatemalan was alone, she would surprise him by driving the spike into his throat. The thought of doing it was repulsive, but the thought of being executed was more so. She had to do it. If she could get a gun to her father, they would have at least a possibility of getting out of the big adobe mansion alive.

When there was no response to her tapping, Lucy repeated it. Then she heard shoe leather scrape on the hallway floor, and a key rattled in the lock. When the door opened, she found herself looking at a man not more than an inch taller than she was and perhaps a year or two older. Smiling at him, she said in a whisper, "Our water jug is empty. Could we get some more?" As she spoke, she stepped out past the threshold and flicked a glance in both directions. The guard was indeed alone. Her heart quickened.

It was obvious from the look in the young Guatemalan's eyes that while he considered her an enemy, he did admire her beauty. Smiling back, he said, "I am not allowed to leave my post, señorita. You will have to wait until morning for more water."

Lucy could feel the pulsebeat of her temples as she gripped the spike tightly under her sleeve. Suddenly she lashed out with her hand, holding the spike as she would a knife, ready to drive it into the guard's throat. But the well-trained guerrilla sensed her move, and he raised an arm to protect himself. The point of the spike merely cut through his shirt and gouged his arm.

Before she could make another stab at him, his fist

caught her square on the jaw with a solid punch. Lucy slammed into the doorjamb and then collapsed on the floor. Immediately two guerrillas came bounding down the hall from the front part of the house.

Hearing the commotion, Duncan Campbell awoke, and when he saw the door standing open, he leapt from the bed. He gasped when he saw his daughter lying unconscious at the guard's feet. Patricia stirred when she heard him running toward the door in his bare feet, shouting, "Lucy! Lucy!"

The guard was holding his bleeding arm as the other two Guatemalans drew up, and he quickly told what had happened. Shoving the man out of the way, Duncan Campbell dropped to his knees beside Lucy, rubbing her hands briskly. Looking up with angry eyes at the bleeding guard, he snapped, "What did you do to my daughter? Why is this door open?"

Lucy moaned and rolled her head back and forth as the guard leaned over and picked up the spike from the floor. Pointing the sharp end at Campbell, he hissed through his teeth, "It is open because your daughter tricked me—and then she tried to stab me with this! I hit her to defend myself."

One of the other guerrillas scowled and said, "Señor Campbell, you had best instruct your daughter not to try anything foolish again. If she does, she will pay with her life."

Campbell helped the unsteady young woman to her feet and then asked, "Lucy, what were you trying to do?"

Responding groggily, she told him what she had attempted and why.

He shook his head slowly. "Ah, my girl. Though your attempt was foolish, I admire you for it." With an arm around her shoulder, he guided her through the door and said, "Come on, honey. Let's try to get some sleep."

When the door was shut behind them, leaving the Campbells alone in the moonlit room, Patricia embraced her daughter and admonished her, saying, "Lucy, you might have been killed."

"I had to try, Mother. I had to try."

"You're a brave one, I'll say that for you," Patricia breathed. "Far braver than I."

"It wasn't bravery," Lucy said softly. "It was pure desperation. And I was scared to death." She sighed, adding, "I'm not going to give up. I'm not."

The next morning, May 14, Rondo Ortega and U.S. Marshal John McCain dismounted in front of the Alegre Viaje Stage Line office in Chihuahua and went inside. There they found the rotund, squat Julio Herrera behind the counter working on his financial records. He smiled at the two men as they entered, and after acknowledging Ortega, he extended his hand over the counter and said, "*Buenos días*, Marshal McCain. I am sorry I was not here when you arrived yesterday."

Gripping the man's chubby hand, McCain replied, "A person can't be in two places at once, can he?"

"Sometimes I wish I could," Herrera responded, chuckling. He shook his head, and his shock of thick, black, curly hair waggled just above his bushy eyebrows.

At that moment Herrera's assistant, Rubin Lupino, came in through the back door of the office and greeted Ortega and McCain with a wide smile.

"I'd like to discuss my plans with you, Señor Herrera," said McCain.

"Certainly, Marshal. Why don't we sit down and talk. Rubin, close the door so we will have some privacy."

The young man did as he was told and then sat down with the other three.

"So, what are your plans, Marshal?" Herrera asked amiably.

"You are aware that Ray Gonzales has volunteered to supply the manpower I will need to overcome the guerrillas and rescue the Campbells?"

"*Sí.*"

"I plan to make my move on the mansion three days from now, the morning of the seventeenth . . . two days before the deadline set by the guerrillas. Then the Campbells will be put aboard a company stagecoach."

"*Sí.* That is a good plan."

"I figure we'll have to kill every Guatemalan at the mansion when we go in. We don't dare let one live and take the chance he could get away and run to another guerrilla stronghold for help. This operation has got to be kept as secret as possible."

Rubin Lupino asked, "Señor McCain, how early in the morning do you plan to make the assault on the mansion?"

"At sunup," came the reply. "Why do you ask?"

"Our next regular stage to Juárez leaves about thirty minutes past noon on the seventeenth. Do you want to put the Campbells on that one?"

"I'm not sure, Rubin," responded the marshal. "I'll need to think about it a little. We'll take the Campbells to Rondo's barn for safekeeping immediately after we free them from the guerrillas." He paused and then said, "When is the next regular run to Juárez after that?"

"At the exact same time two days later," replied Lupino.

McCain nodded. "I'll let you know tomorrow or the next day what my plans are." Looking at Herrera, he asked, "Is this going to cause a problem for you? We won't want anyone except Gonzales's men and myself on the coach that carries the Campbells."

"We will work around it," Herrera assured him. "At present we have only two passengers booked on the coach leaving the seventeenth for Juárez and none on the one leaving the nineteenth. For the time being, we will not book anyone on the coach for the nineteenth. We can always tell people it is full."

"I certainly appreciate your cooperation, Señor Herrera," McCain said. "And believe me, my countrymen appreciate it, too."

"It is our pleasure to help," replied Herrera with a warm smile. "Incidentally, I take it that you will not need our driver and shotgun man?"

"No. I think it best that I use Ray Gonzales's men all the way. I am curious, though. How many stagecoaches does your company run?"

"We have six on the road at all times, Marshal. Chihuahua is the hub of our operations, and we run coaches west to Hermosillo, south to Torreón, and of course north to Juárez."

Pondering the information, McCain asked, "Do you keep any spare coaches, in case one breaks down?"

"Of course. We have three extra ones in our barn out back."

"I see. And are they all painted and lettered as fancy as the one I rode from Juárez?"

"Sí. Rubin has done the work on all of them. He also is very good at repairing them."

Rubin Lupino beamed with pleasure when McCain said to him, "You do excellent work, Rubin. The coach I rode in was very attractive."

"*Gracias, Señor McCain,*" replied Lupino, his smile widening. "I try to do a good job for the stage line."

John McCain thanked Julio Herrera once again and then stood and said, "Rondo, we need to get going. I want to talk to the telegrapher."

The men all shook hands, and then McCain and Ortega stepped out into the morning heat, walking past a few doors until they came to the telegraph office. As they entered, the telegrapher looked up from his desk behind the counter and, standing, approached them. After the two Mexicans had greeted each other, Ortega introduced Noe Lujan to McCain, identifying him as the U.S. marshal who had come to free the U.S. secretary of war and his family from the Guatemalan guerrillas.

Noe Lujan, a small, wiry man in his late fifties, smiled and said, "It is a pleasure to meet you, Señor McCain. I have been expecting you."

McCain's eyebrows arched. "You have?"

"Sí. I have relayed many messages from your government officials to the guerrillas at the mansion. Along with these, a message came from the American officials to me."

"Is that right?" McCain asked. "So our people are entrusting you with all the information about my mission?"

"Sí," Lujan replied. "Rondo has told your Chief Eldridge Harris in El Paso about me, and he in turn informed your government officials that they can trust me."

"Then I'm sure I can, too," McCain remarked, smiling. "I need some information, and I need your help."

"I will do anything I can," Lujan responded.

Confident that the telegrapher was absolutely trustworthy, John McCain took a few minutes to tell Noe Lujan of his plan to rescue the Campbell family on May 17 and transport them to Juárez by stagecoach. Then he asked, "Who receives the Guatemalans' messages in New Orleans?"

"A man named Jorge Lucero, Marshal," replied Lujan. "He is some kind of Guatemalan government official—a diplomat or something like that—who happened to be in New Orleans at the time of the shooting. Apparently he wired Presidente Cresada about the incident and the arrests. Lucero's messages come to me, and I pass them on to the guerrillas at the mansion, using a messenger."

He suddenly grinned and explained, "They believe that I think they are merely guards protecting a very rich and very private magnate—they do not know that our authorities found out the truth. Understand, Marshal, their messages are written in code, and they contain no mention of the Campbells or the Guatemalan prisoners in New Orleans. They are very careful about that."

Clapping the telegrapher on the back, John McCain said admiringly, "You're a good man to have in our corner, that's for sure. By the way, how *do* the guerrillas send messages to Lucero?"

"If they want to reply to the wire, a man named José Gristo writes the message down and sends it back with the messenger. Gristo is the apparent leader. A tough hombre, I understand."

"So how do they work it if they want to send a message at a time other than when your messenger is there?"

"Gristo sends a man into town. He is a very confident one, I will give him that. He does not worry about his men's being seen—but, of course, he feels secure in his act. They have things well planned. If the guerrillas at the mansion do not get the message by dawn on the nineteenth that their *compadres* have been released, the Campbells will be summarily executed."

McCain thought a moment and then asked, "Noe, what if we were to have your messenger deliver a false wire . . . one that says the prisoners in New Orleans have been released?"

"It would not work, Señor McCain," Lujan replied quickly. "You see, I am sure that every message passing between Lucero in New Orleans and Gristo at the mansion contains a secret code word—and I do not know which word it is. If we were to send a message to José Gristo that did not contain that secret word, the Campbells would probably be executed."

John McCain removed his hat, ran his fingers through his dark, wavy hair and growled, "Those guerrillas are clever, aren't they?"

"Too clever," put in Rondo Ortega. "It seems to me they have done this kind of thing before."

"They're not beginners, that's for sure," commented McCain. Then he asked Lujan, "Who's been carrying the messages to the mansion for you?"

"Whoever I can find around town to take them out there for me," the telegrapher answered. "So far I have used three different men."

"Good!" exclaimed McCain. "That means the guerrillas won't think anything of it if you use yet another man, right?"

"I would not think so. Am I assuming correctly that you are going to be the new man?"

"Correct," McCain confirmed. "Now, did I understand you to say there have been messages relayed from the American officials to José Gristo?"

"Sí. There have been three so far. Each one has been to report encouraging news to Gristo, making him believe progress is being made toward the release of the nine Guatemalans. Of course, these messages have actually been sent to play for time, stalling until you could engineer the rescue."

The federal lawman digested this information for a moment and then instructed, "Here's what I want you to do. Send a wire to the American authorities in New Orleans and tell them that I want two more encouraging messages to come through to Gristo—one tomorrow morning and one at dawn on the morning of the seventeenth."

"All right," Lujan confirmed, writing it down on a piece of paper.

"I want to be the bearer of both these messages to Gristo."

"But you are not a Mexican, Señor McCain," put in Rondo Ortega. "Will this not make José Gristo suspicious?"

"I don't think so," he responded. "My hair and mustache are as dark as yours, so I think I can pass for one of your people." He smiled. "And my Spanish is quite good, besides."

Ortega and Lujan looked at each other and then shrugged. The telegrapher told the marshal, "I will wire the American authorities with your message, and I will be expecting you on both mornings."

"Good. Now, let me give you a message to send to Chief Marshal Harris in El Paso. I want to let him know how things are progressing up to this point."

After writing the message, John McCain left the telegraph office with Rondo Ortega. As they walked toward their horses, McCain said, "I need to meet with Ray Gonzales as soon as possible."

"He is supposed to be at my place in the morning," Ortega promised.

"Good. I figure I'll need fifteen or sixteen tough fighting men to help me carry out the assault on the mansion—and of those, four will also assist me on the journey north."

"I am sure Ray can provide you with what you need in the way of men, Marshal. Is there anything else you will require?"

"Yes. A dozen sticks of dynamite. Can you get those for me?"

"I know exactly where I will get them," responded the Mexican. "I have a friend in the mining business."

"Good. The next request may not be as easy."

"And what is that?" asked Ortega.

"Four female dogs in heat."

Ortega's brow furrowed. "I do not understand, Marshal."

"I'll explain it later," McCain promised, grinning. "Do you think you can do it?"

"Four female dogs will not be a problem," replied Ortega. "Four female dogs in heat . . . this I cannot guarantee. But I will do my best."

"That's all I can ask," McCain responded. "While you're doing that, I'll be in the hiding place at the barn, polishing up my plans."

The sun had gone down and twilight was settling over Chihuahua when Rondo Ortega descended the ladder into the barn cellar. U.S. Marshal John McCain was sitting at the table, studying by lantern light the notes that he had written. Looking up as the Mexican entered, McCain said, "I think I've got it planned as close to perfect as possible, my good friend. How did you do?"

The little man smiled broadly. "You will be pleased to know that I have the dynamite you requested, and four female dogs . . . all in heat."

"Very good!" exclaimed McCain.

"And Gonzales and sixteen tough hombres will be here tomorrow morning." Gesturing toward the ladder, he then suggested, "It is dinner time. Come join me."

While the two men were eating supper, Ortega said, "All right, *mi amigo,* my curiosity can wait no longer. Tell me what you are going to do with the female dogs."

"They are going to help me create a diversion," explained McCain. "Just before Ray Gonzales and his men launch the attack, one man will be driving a wagon down the road past the mansion. The caged dogs will be in the back. The guards no doubt will be watching him. He will pretend to have trouble with the wagon, and when he stops, he'll get the dogs to bark, thereby drawing the attention of the male Dobermans behind the gate. When the Dobermans begin to show excitement, the man will 'accidentally' let the females out of their cages." McCain grinned, adding, "You know what will happen."

Ortega threw his head back and laughed heartily. "*Sí.* Those boy dogs will be desperate to get to the girl dogs! That will keep the guards busy!"

"Exactly. At the same time, Gonzales and his bunch will gallop out of the woods and then leap the walls with their guns blazing."

"The diversion with the dogs will make it much easier for them," agreed Ortega, nodding vigorously.

"You've got the picture," McCain said wryly.

"Now, what about the dynamite?"

"That's for the riflemen on the roof. Protected as they are by that low wall that runs around the perimeter of the roof, we can't shoot them from the ground. I'll have two of Gonzales's men hiding under a tarp in the back of the wagon that carries the dogs. When the attack begins, they'll toss short-fused sticks of dynamite onto the roof and take out the riflemen."

Ortega laughed again. "You think of everything, John!"

McCain was silent for a moment and then said, "There's just one problem."

"What is that?"

"If the Campbells are being kept on the second floor of the mansion, the exploding dynamite could harm them. We've got to find out exactly where they are."

Nodding, Ortega suggested, "There is only one way to find that out. We will have to capture one of the guerrillas and make him tell us."

"That's what I was thinking," replied the federal lawman. "It's too bad I didn't think of that sooner. I could have perhaps forced one of those guards I killed yesterday to give us the information we need."

Nodding in agreement, Ortega put down his tortilla and then asked, "Do you suppose those two were part of a regular patrol outside the walls? Certainly if they had spotted you from behind the walls, the other guards would have known they were going after you. We'll just have to capture another of them."

"That makes sense," McCain responded, slapping his palm on the top of the table. "We'll wait in the woods near the mansion at dawn—and one way or another we'll grab us a guerrilla and squeeze the information out of him if we have to."

Chapter Four

On the morning of May 15, with dawn still only a thin line of gray on the eastern horizon, U.S. Marshal John McCain and Rondo Ortega dismounted in the woods north of the big adobe mansion. There they left their horses, as well as a spare mount they had brought along to carry the Guatemalan guerrilla they hoped to capture and bring back to Ortega's barn.

Pressing through the trees, they walked around to the east and reached the edge of the forest, from where they could clearly see the mansion in the growing light. They watched as guerrillas filed out the front door of the mansion and gathered near the wrought iron gate.

"Look!" Ortega whispered hoarsely as he pointed toward a group of men coming through the woods to the east of the mansion.

Nodding, McCain remarked, "Just as we thought. They've got men patrolling regularly on foot, and it looks as though they're changing patrol personnel right now."

Four guerrillas approached the gate from the east while at the same time two more came out of the forest to the west of the mansion. McCain assessed the entire area, looking for additional men to appear, but there were no more.

Some of the dogs fussed and barked as the gate swung open, and six men stepped out to meet the six who were

51

coming in. While they paused to talk to each other, John McCain said to Rondo Ortega, "Looks like six is their number."

"Sí," replied Rondo. "And it looks like they patrol in pairs."

"Mm-hmm. If that's the case, we'll have to capture two instead of one."

The eastern sky was showing pink when the guerrillas who were now on patrol duty left the gate and began to spread in three directions. One pair headed in a beeline toward the spot where McCain and Ortega were nestled among the trees.

"Good!" whispered McCain. "They're going to come right to us! Let's back a bit farther into the trees. Let them get totally out of sight of the mansion before we jump them."

As they retreated deeper into the woods, Ortega asked, "How should we work it?"

"We'll have to watch them real close and keep ourselves directly in front of them as they enter the forest. When we can determine the exact direction they're taking, we'll hide behind trees, let them pass . . . then jump them. Use the barrel of your revolver to knock your man unconscious. It's vitally important that we don't let them make any sound that would alert their compatriots back at the mansion."

"I understand," Ortega assured the lawman.

Peering through the dense forest, McCain and Ortega watched the two guerrillas cross the open area and enter the woods. Together they backtracked, swinging to their right a few yards so as to remain directly ahead of the approaching patrolmen.

Once the course was evident, McCain pointed to a large tree a few feet to his right. Ortega leapt behind it, pulling his revolver. The marshal then chose a tree a short distance from Ortega's and stood behind it, easing his gun from its holster. The two Guatemalans were conversing casually, and it was clear they were going to pass directly between McCain and Ortega.

The guerrillas drew abreast of the two hidden men and then moved past them. Springing like a cougar, John McCain was immediately on his man. He cracked the guerrilla solidly on the head, and the man's knees buckled and he fell to the ground.

Rondo Ortega was one step behind his target when the guerrilla heard the rustling of dried leaves on the floor of the forest. He had started to turn around when the Mexican brought down his revolver, slamming him on the cheekbone. The Guatemalan staggered but did not fall, and although his eyes were slightly glazed, he was bringing up his rifle for action. Moving in quickly, Ortega brought the revolver down savagely on the man's temple, and the man collapsed in a heap.

When the unconscious guerrillas were tied and gagged, McCain and Ortega carried them quickly through the trees and draped them over the back of the spare horse. Within twenty minutes, they had ridden into Ortega's yard and drawn up beside the barn. Both guerrillas were now fully conscious, and squealing through the gags in their mouths and fighting their bonds, they were dragged through the barn and lowered into the cellar.

Placed on the floor in the center of the large room, the captives' hands were left tied behind their backs as the gags were removed from their mouths. Both men rolled to a sitting position and began swearing profusely, making all kinds of threats.

John McCain stood over them and shouted, "Shut up!" When they had complied, albeit with their evident rage undiminished, McCain announced, "Now, you are going to answer my questions about your hideout!"

One of the guerrillas was a bit larger and meaner looking than his partner. Glaring at McCain, he snapped, "You are wasting your time, *gringo*. Whoever you are, we are not telling you anything!"

The muscles in McCain's jaw tightened. Standing over the man and regarding him with flashing eyes, he warned, "You're going to tell me what I want to know, mister! It can come easy or it can come hard—the choice is yours—but I'm going to get it out of you, that's a promise. Now, I want to know where in the mansion the Campbells are being kept. And I want to know how many guerrillas there are at the mansion."

The prisoners looked at each other, then the larger one retorted gratingly and insolently, "We refuse to answer any of your questions."

The marshal knelt down to their level and stared intently at the one who had spoken, saying heatedly, "I will say this only one more time: I *am* going to find out what I want to know. I don't want to have to rough you up, but I will. Now, where in the mansion are the Campbells being held?"

The larger guerrilla suddenly shot a foot out at McCain, attempting to kick him in the face. The agile lawman dodged the foot and then grabbed it with strong hands. Gritting his teeth, he gave it a violent twist, snapping the bone. The guerrilla howled, going limp, and his smaller cohort suddenly regarded the marshal fearfully.

Rising to his feet, McCain snarled at the injured man, who was moaning in pain, "All right, pal, answer my questions immediately or I'll get rougher."

The guerrilla's words crackled with hatred, "No matter what you do to us, we will never tell you what you want to know! Never!" Glancing at his partner, his eyes contained a warning as he added stiffly, "We have taken an oath of loyalty to Presidente Cresada and to Guatemala—and nothing you do to us will break that!"

Looking at the smaller man, McCain was relieved to see the fear still in his eyes. Turning to Ortega, he ordered, "Rondo, open the door of that storeroom over there."

As the Mexican promptly did as he was told, the injured

guerrilla looked at McCain and asked, "What are you going to do?"

Bending down and grabbing him by the shirt collar, the marshal dragged him toward the door that Ortega now held open and sardonically growled, "I refuse to answer your question."

With a powerful thrust, McCain heaved the man through the door. The momentum carried the Guatemalan all the way to the wall, which he slammed into with great force. He howled when the broken leg tangled beneath him, bearing his weight as he fell. Then, swearing vehemently, he began kicking the wall with his good leg, making as much disturbance as possible.

Glaring at the man, John McCain sighed and stepped into the storeroom, saying, "I really do hate to hit a man when his hands are tied behind his back, but I've had enough." Bending over, he hoisted up the captive with his left hand and unleashed a hard blow to the man's jaw. The guerrilla's eyes glazed, but he tried to fight back. McCain hit him again, this time with greater force, and the prisoner went limp as his eyes rolled back in their sockets. McCain dropped him in a heap and stepped out of the room, saying, "Lock it, Rondo."

Ortega dashed to a small cupboard, pulled open a drawer, and drew out a skeleton key. While Ortega was locking the storeroom door, John McCain stood over the smaller Guatemalan and remarked, "You look like you may have more sense than your friend. What's your name?"

Perspiration was beaded on the guerrilla's brow. There was even more fear in his eyes than before. His mouth moved silently for a moment before his voice would come. Then he mumbled, "Juan. Juan Jaramillo."

"And what is the name of your stubborn friend?"

"Pedro Garcia."

Kneeling down so as to look the hostage in the eye, the marshal asked levelly, "Juan Jaramillo, how would you like two broken arms?"

"I . . . I would not like that, *señor*."

"Well, for starters, that's what you're going to get unless you cooperate better than your *compadre* did, because I'm out of patience. Now, are you going to answer my questions, or do I first need to convince you that I mean business?"

Juan Jaramillo's dark face, frozen with fear, told McCain that the man was already convinced.

Rising to his full height, the federal marshal barked, "Well?"

"The . . . the Campbells are being held in a ground-floor bedroom," sputtered Jaramillo, looking up with bulging eyes at the towering man.

"All three of them?"

"*Sí.*"

"Which bedroom?" McCain demanded, glad to know dynamite could be used to take out the riflemen on the roof without danger of harming the Campbells.

"It is the second from the front on the south side."

"Are they tied up?"

"No. They are free to move about the room."

"How many guerrillas are there at the mansion?"

"There were thirty of us at first, but two of our men disappeared the day before yesterday. With Pedro and me gone, there are now twenty-six of us."

Giving Juan Jaramillo a wolfish grin, McCain looked down at him and said tightly, "I'm in a position where I have to take your word, Juan. You are telling me the truth, aren't you? I mean, if I should attack the mansion and find out there are more guerrillas than you have told me about, I would be very, very angry. And when I get back here where you'll be locked up, I would break every bone in your body. Not only that, but I would tear off both your arms and beat you to death with them. Do you understand?"

"*Sí, señor!*" the small Guatemalan gasped. "I swear! I have told you the truth!"

"Good. Now, I want you to tell me about José Gristo. He is in charge?"

"*Sí, señor.* José Gristo is the top guerrilla fighter in all Guatemala. Presidente Enrique Cresada chose him especially to capture the Campbell family in order to make the American authorities release the Guatemalans from the prison in Louisiana."

McCain smiled. "Excellent. You have made me very happy, Juan." Turning his head, the lawman said, "Unlock the door, Rondo, and put Juan in with his buddy."

The marshal helped Jaramillo to his feet while Ortega opened the storeroom door. McCain ushered the Guatamalan into the room and then untied his hands. Pedro Garcia had regained consciousness, and he glared first at the lawman and then at his cohort. It was clear that he knew Juan Jaramillo had given the *gringo* the information he wanted, and when he looked at the smaller man, Jaramillo dropped his eyes in shame.

Holding the short length of rope loose in one hand, McCain said, "We will contact the Mexican authorities and have them haul you off to jail. Perhaps, if you are lucky, a doctor will be provided to set your leg, Garcia."

"What about *my* hands, *gringo?*" Garcia demanded, his face reflecting the pain he was enduring.

Shrugging, the marshal answered, "If your pal wants you to have your hands free, he can untie you." With that, McCain stepped out, and Rondo Ortega locked the door and pocketed the key.

Walking across the room toward the ladder, McCain said, "I need to go to town. Have you got a sombrero and some other clothing that I can borrow? I need to look as authentically Mexican as possible."

"Of course," Ortega replied. "You may have to keep your own trousers, shirt, and boots, but I can fix you up with a vest and a sombrero. I can give you Mexican-style spurs also, if you wish."

"Let's go the whole route," McCain responded. "I've

got to do everything I can to convince those guerrillas that I'm Mexican."

It was exactly six-thirty in the morning when U.S. Marshal John McCain rode up in front of the telegraph office and slid from his saddle. The agent, who lived in the apartment above the office, was up and about when the lawman arrived.

Pushing open the office door, McCain was greeted by Noe Lujan, who smiled warmly and said, "Good morning, Señor McCain. The message you requested from New Orleans has arrived already. I have it right here." Reaching into a shirt pocket as he spoke, the telegrapher handed McCain the telegram.

"Thanks, Noe," said the marshal, immediately turning to leave. "I need to deliver this to the mansion and then get back to Rondo's place. Ray Gonzales and his men will be there shortly."

McCain went outside and strode to his horse, vaulting into the saddle. He took a minute to read the telegram, smiled to himself and then touched his spurs to the horse's sides and rode out of Chihuahua.

A quarter of an hour later, John McCain trotted his horse up to the wrought iron gate at the big adobe mansion, and the Dobermans immediately began to bark. The guards quieted them as one of the guerrillas approached the gate and asked in Spanish, "What do you want?"

"I have a telegram," McCain answered, praying his Mexican accent was accurate. "My instructions are that I must deliver it to José Gristo himself." McCain wanted to get a look at Gristo.

The guerrilla's surly face twisted into a sneer, and he countered stubbornly, "I will take it to José."

"No," McCain insisted, shaking his head. "The instructions are that this message must be placed in Gristo's hands by me personally."

Looking annoyed, the Guatemalan muttered to himself

and then headed for the front door of the mansion. The two guards that were walking their dogs back and forth behind the five-foot wall eyed McCain warily but said nothing. Some three or four minutes had passed when the guard returned, followed by a man who McCain presumed was José Gristo.

Stepping up to the gate with irritation written on his dark face, Gristo looked piercingly at McCain and snapped, "Why is it necessary that you deliver the telegram to me? My men can carry it to me!"

Adopting a humble attitude, McCain replied innocently, "Please pardon the inconvenience, Señor Gristo, but the telegraph agent ordered me to deliver it to you personally. I am only doing what I am told."

Extending his hand through the gate, Gristo demanded, "Give it to me!"

McCain placed it between the man's fingers and said in a servile voice, "I hope it is good news for you, Señor Gristo."

The guerrilla leader did not comment. Holding the telegram in his hand, he wheeled and walked briskly back into the mansion.

Smiling to himself, John McCain mounted his horse and trotted back to the road.

It was just before eight o'clock, and Rondo Ortega and John McCain—who was once again wearing his own clothes—were finishing their breakfast in the Ortega kitchen when galloping hooves were heard coming into the yard. Ortega set his coffee cup down, rose, and declared, "That will be Ray Gonzales and his men."

Ortega and McCain stepped out onto the back porch to see a band of hard-faced, tough-looking Mexicans riding up to the house. Ray Gonzales, who was in the lead, rode a coal-black gelding and was totally dressed in black as well. The only relief from the dark monochrome came from the silver studs adorning the double-holstered black

gun belt he wore and the pearl handles on his twin Colt
.45s. As he reined in at the porch, Gonzales pushed the
big black sombrero off his head so that it hung down from
the back of his neck by its chin strap.

Smiling broadly and showing his mouthful of large white
teeth, Gonzales greeted Ortega and dismounted. The thick-
bodied Mexican was introduced to John McCain, and when
the two men shook hands, McCain was impressed by the
strength in Gonzales's grip. The man stood no more than
five feet eight inches, but McCain guessed he weighed a
solid, muscular two hundred pounds. His black eyes flashed
with vitality and eagerness as he said, "Well, Señor McCain,
we are here to do your bidding. Now tell me what it is you
wish us to do."

John McCain gazed slowly at the faces of the other
riders, counting sixteen of them in all. They were rugged
men, all right—and armed to the teeth. McCain was more
impressed with their leader, however. Ray Gonzales, who
was in his early forties, looked tougher than any of his
followers. His face was scarred in several places, giving
mute testimony to the fact that the man had fought many a
battle.

While the other riders dismounted and took their ease
in the yard, Ray Gonzales followed John McCain and
Rondo Ortega into the barn. They descended into the
cellar and, by lantern light, sat at the table while McCain
laid out his plan. While they were talking, they heard a
muffled cry and scuffling sounds coming from the storeroom.

Gonzales looked toward the closed door and asked,
"What is that?"

Ortega quickly explained about the two captured Guatemalan guerrillas. "They seem to be having a dispute," he
commented.

There were more scuffling sounds, a gagging noise, and
then a thump. McCain rose to his feet and suggested,
"We'd better take a look, Rondo."

McCain and Rondo Ortega hurried across the room.

When Ortega turned the key and pulled the door open, both the lawman and the Mexican gasped. Glaring out at his captors, the length of rope that had bound his hands dangling from one hand, Pedro Garcia was breathing hard and leaning over the lifeless form of Juan Jaramillo. Jaramillo had been strangled.

Before McCain could speak, Garcia sneered at the marshal and spat, "That traitor got what he deserved for cooperating with our enemies!" While the words were coming out of his mouth, Garcia reached toward McCain, grabbing for the gun on the lawman's hip.

McCain sidestepped him, but Garcia then used his momentum to snatch the gun from Rondo Ortega's holster instead. Limping quickly through the storeroom door, the guerrilla wheeled, about to fire at both men. Ray Gonzales instantly stood and whipped out his right-hand revolver, but before he could use it, John McCain drew his Colt .45 and fired.

The sharp roar echoed off the walls of the cellar, and blue-white gun smoke filled the room. Pedro Garcia sprawled on the floor faceup, a bullet in his heart.

As he dropped his gun back in his studded holster, Gonzales gazed with admiration at the lawman and declared, "You are plenty fast with that weapon, Señor McCain."

"Have to be in my business," the marshal responded drily.

The shot brought immediate action from Gonzales's men, and a number of them raced into the barn and stood around the opening in the floor. Adding to the commotion of the men all shouting at once, trying to find out what had happened, the female dogs that were penned up in a stall at the rear of the barn began barking loudly.

Calling for quiet, Gonzales explained what had occurred and instructed a couple of his men to take the bodies out of the cellar for burial. The rest of them were to wait outside. Then, when all was quiet, Gonzales again gave

John McCain his complete attention while the marshal finished detailing his plans.

After the entire scheme had been presented, Ray Gonzales smiled broadly, agreeing with everything, and suggested that McCain now inform the rest of the men personally of what was expected of them. The three men climbed out of the cellar and gathered the group at the back porch of the house.

Standing before the crowd of fighters, John McCain reiterated his plan to rescue the Campbells and return them to Juárez by stagecoach, and then he filled them in on the details, including how the penned female dogs would be used to divert the Dobermans.

After McCain had gone over everything carefully, Ray Gonzales pointed into the group and said, "Trinidad Cardenas, you have had the most experience with animals. I want you to handle the wagon and the dogs."

Cardenas was chewing on an unlit cigar. He shoved it to one corner of his mouth and then smiled and nodded.

Turning to Gonzales, John McCain said, "I need you to choose four men to ride the stagecoach with me all the way to Juárez—and I need them chosen immediately so I can begin schooling them for the trip. Two will serve as driver and shotgun guard, and the other two will ride as passengers inside the coach with the Campbells and myself."

"I have just the man for the driver, Marshal," Gonzales responded. "Antonio Barillo. He has driven a stagecoach in the past."

"Excellent," McCain said.

Gonzales then chose Alonzo Montoya as shotgun guard. Montoya was a big, husky man and skilled with all kinds of guns. McCain was pleased with the looks of him.

Turning to McCain, Gonzales told him, "I have decided that I will be one of the men who rides inside the coach, Marshal."

"That's fine, Ray," McCain agreed. "I was hoping that you would do that. Who else will ride inside?"

Gonzales pointed to a mean-eyed, tough-looking man who stood on the fringe of the group and said, "Manuel Ramos, you will be the other passenger."

As Ramos nodded his assent, McCain commented, "He looks tough enough."

"Believe me," Gonzales said wryly, "he is."

In turn looking each man in the group in the eye, U.S. Marshal John McCain advised them that they would all meet at the barn two hours before dawn on the seventeenth for last-minute preparations. He then dismissed the men, except for those who would be riding the stage. They were briefed on their hazardous journey north—and instructed to get a good night's rest before the trip.

The next morning—May 16—John McCain and Rondo Ortega visited the Alegre Viaje Stage Line office for a final conference with Julio Herrera and Rubin Lupino. Immediately after the men had greeted each other, Lupino asked, "Have you decided which run you want to use for your purposes, Señor McCain?"

"Yes, Rubin," replied the marshal. "I think it would be safer to let one stage take its regular run after we have freed the Campbells. I have instructed the men who are going to attack the mansion that all the guerrillas there must be killed, but if word of the rescue should somehow reach other Guatemalan guerrillas nearby, they might decide to check out the first regularly scheduled stagecoach. If they do, they won't find the Campbells aboard—and I'm hoping that this will make the next run less suspicious. Meanwhile, the Guatemalans will be scouring the hill country between here and Juárez, looking for a group of riders attempting to escort the Campbells out of the country by the back roads."

Lupino and Herrera agreed that McCain's idea made good sense. The marshal then laid out the details of his plan, explaining about Ray Gonzales and the three other men who would be on the stage.

At that moment two prospective passengers, a man and a woman, came in to book passage to Hermosillo. Leaving Rubin Lupino to wait on them, Julio Herrera led McCain and Ortega out to the barn behind the office to show them the stagecoach that would actually be carrying the Campbells to Juárez.

Gesturing proudly at the brilliantly painted coach, the doors of which were hanging open, Herrera told the lawman excitedly, "I have had Rubin working on it day and night, Señor McCain. It is almost finished. Take a look at the inside."

McCain peeked in and saw that the doors had been plated with a quarter-inch of iron on the back side. "Very nice work, Señor Herrera. Very nice indeed."

Smiling, Herrera explained, "I had this done so that in the event of gunplay, the Campbells can get down on the floor of the coach and be relatively safe."

"I'll be sure to tell the Campbells of the extra effort you have made on their behalf. As a matter of fact, I'll see to it that President Cleveland himself knows what you've done."

"The *americanos* are my friends," Herrera said warmly. "It is my pleasure to help in this small way."

Studying the inside of the coach for a moment, McCain then asked Ortega, "Rondo, can you get me a few more sticks of dynamite, aside from the ones we'll be using at the mansion?"

"Of course. How many do you want?"

"Six . . . maybe eight."

"What are you going to do with them?"

"Nothing, I hope. I just want them along on the trip in case I have to ward off attackers. It never hurts to have a little surprise firepower."

Ortega grinned and shook his head. "Remind me never to get on your bad side, John."

McCain chuckled and then said to Herrera, "We're all set, then. The Campbells will be kept in Rondo's secret cellar until just before noon on the nineteenth. Then we'll bring them here in Rondo's wagon and board them in front of your office as if they're regular passengers. I want to keep things looking as normal as possible."

"Fine, Señor McCain," Herrera responded. "We will be ready."

McCain shook Herrera's hand and then turned to leave, with Ortega following. When McCain reached the door of the barn, Herrera called, "Good luck at the mansion, Señor McCain. I hope it all goes as you have planned it."

John McCain turned and looked back over his shoulder. With a grim look in his dark-brown eyes, he responded, "It has to, Señor Herrera. It just has to."

Chapter Five

When U.S. Marshal John McCain rode back into Rondo Ortega's yard an hour before dawn on May 17, reining the horse beneath him to a stop, he glanced around and smiled. All was obviously ready for the assault on the Guatemalan hideout.

Trinidad Cardenas was seated on the wagon seat, holding the reins of the team. In the back of the wagon, two men lay in the wagon bed, their lower torsos already covered by a tarp. The female dogs whined nervously in their pen, and the men were speaking soothingly to them. Ray Gonzales and the rest of the fighters were sitting astride their mounts, clearly impatient to get started.

Gonzales peered through the gloom and asked, "Do you have it?"

Patting a pocket of the Mexican vest he wore, McCain answered, "Right here . . . complete with the demand that the bearer of the telegram be allowed to enter the mansion and talk with the Campbells."

McCain took a few minutes to go over the plan briefly one more time. When there were no questions from the men, he said, "All right, we're ready to go."

From his place on the porch, Rondo Ortega called, "John, are you sure I should not come along? It would not hurt to have one more gun."

"I appreciate your offer, Rondo," replied McCain, "but

it's best that you remain here. These men are trained fighters; you are not."

"All right," agreed Ortega. "I will be ready to care for the Campbells when you bring them. Good luck."

"Thanks. We'll need it." McCain then touched spurs to his horse's flanks and commanded, "Let's go!"

The first light of dawn was glowing on the earth's eastern edge as the assault team approached the mansion. John McCain drew rein, and the rest of the riders and the wagoneer did likewise. Facing the men, the U.S. marshal said, "Now, as I told you, this has to be timed perfectly. The patrol personnel do their change just at sunup. I'll ride in as they meet at the gate. I'm going to try and pique their curiosity about this telegram so that they'll delay going out on patrol—at least long enough to put our plan into action.

"Stay just close enough behind me to be able to keep me in sight, and when you see me ride in, take your places." Addressing the wagoneer, McCain added, "Trinidad, the moment you see me enter the house, drive at a normal pace down the road. I'll need a little time after I get inside to be in a position to protect the Campbells. Okay?

"*Sí*," Cardenas replied.

John McCain adjusted the huge sombrero on his head and nudged his mount toward the mansion. Riding cautiously, he held the horse to a walk until he could see by the growing light that the twelve patrolmen were at the gate, obviously making the normal change. The men who were about to begin patrol seemed ready to leave. Sighing with relief that everything was going as scheduled, McCain put the animal into a trot and aimed for the entrance.

The Dobermans set up a furious barking, and the guerrillas glared suspiciously at McCain as he drew up to the gate. The lawman's heart was drumming against his ribs as he told them in Spanish, "I have an important telegram for José Gristo."

A guard, who had been at the gate two days earlier, sternly declared, "This time I will take the telegram to José."

"Ah, but no!" countered McCain, putting a note of mystery into his voice. "This telegram is even more specific than the one I brought two days ago. I must give it to him personally!"

Clearly curious as to the contents of the telegram, and perhaps wondering whether the message bore the information they had been waiting to hear—that their comrades had been released—the patrolmen who had been about to leave moved back within the walls. The head guard assessed McCain for a moment and then pivoted and hurried inside the mansion.

Within half a minute, an angry José Gristo stormed through the door and walked stiffly to the gate, followed by the guard who had gone for him. Peering angrily between the bars at the "Mexican" on horseback, he growled, "What is this nonsense about your having to deliver these telegrams to me in person? The other messengers have not done this!"

"That is because none of them were agents of the United States government, sent to make sure the Campbells are still alive and well."

His face darkening, Gristo glared at his men and swore furiously. Then, clearly enraged that his group's whereabouts had been discovered, he stood and stared at John McCain for a few moments before tearing open the telegram and reading it through. Gristo's face stiffened, and he roared, "This is preposterous! I am not about to let you see the prisoners!"

McCain answered loudly, "If you do not obey this message, your *presidente*'s son will never be released! I certainly would not want to be in your boots when Presidente Cresada hears that his son will die in prison because you would not cooperate with the American officials!"

There was a stirring among the Guatemalans, and it was

apparent that they disagreed with their leader. Nervously, José Gristo barked the names of several of his men. They went to him, and then they walked out of earshot of the others. McCain held his breath as Gristo conferred with them. They gesticulated wildly for a few minutes, and then they moved back to the gate and the rebel leader asked McCain, "What is your name?"

The marshal immediately replied, "John McCain."

"Well, McCain," Gristo said coldly, "I have decided to take you inside and let you talk to the Campbells."

"Now we are getting somewhere," McCain announced, swinging from his saddle. "And, incidentally, if you are thinking of killing me, I would not advise it. If my superiors do not hear from me within an hour, they will begin executing your fellow countrymen held in New Orleans." McCain hoped it was not too obvious a lie, but he was unable to think of any other way to gain a few minutes' time—until his assault plan would go into action.

The guards had to hold the snarling Dobermans at bay as John McCain passed through the gate and followed José Gristo toward the house. Then suddenly the dogs began barking furiously, tugging toward the road, and their handlers seemed to be having trouble controlling them. As the lawman stepped inside the mansion, he smiled to himself. It was clear that Trinidad Cardenas was getting into range with the female dogs.

The door closed behind John McCain, and a few moments later Trinidad Cardenas drove the wagon slowly past the mansion and stopped just beyond the gate. Climbing down from the wagon seat, he glanced over and saw two dogs pawing at the ironwork in a desperate attempt to get out. Cardenas then looked up at the mansion's flat roof where three of the riflemen were trying to catch a glimpse of what was causing the dogs to bark.

The other Dobermans inside the wall came running, having broken free of their handlers, and set up a din of yapping. All the guards were trying futilely to pull the

animals away from the gate. One of the guerrillas peered
through the gate and shouted angrily at Cardenas, who
was stooped on the far side of the wagon, acting as though
he was trying to repair something. Cardenas shouted back
above the barking of the now-frenzied female dogs, "My
wagon is broken down! I will fix it as soon as I can!"

As Cardenas hobbled slowly toward the back of the
wagon, he cast a glance toward the forest north of the
mansion, seeing the shadows of the riders who were poised
and ready to attack.

Behind the gate there was a complete melee, with all
eight male dogs barking loudly and fighting off the men
who were trying to subdue them. One dog tried to leap
the wall and was caught in the nick of time by one of the
guerrillas. Smiling to himself, Trinidad Cardenas surreptitiously opened the door of the pen, releasing the females.
All four immediately bolted, leaping from the wagon and
charging up to the gate. Suddenly what had been total
confusion was absolute bedlam.

"Now!" Cardenas hissed loudly to the men under the
tarp.

The two Mexicans threw back the tarp and rolled over
the side of the wagon bed. Dynamite sticks were jammed
under their belts and wooden matches were pressed between their lips. Quickly, Cardenas reached into the wagon
bed and grabbed a couple of dynamite sticks as well. Each
man struck a match and lit a short fuse.

Ray Gonzales and his riders had been instructed to wait
at the edge of the forest until they saw the fuses being lit.
The moment the matches flared, Trinidad Cardenas faintly
heard Gonzales's command, "Charge!" The guerrillas at
the mansion were so intent on controlling the male dogs
that they were unaware of the riders thundering toward
the north wall.

Cardenas and his companions glanced at each other,
then tossed the dynamite sticks onto the roof. The wagoneer
could see several of the men on the roof momentarily

freeze in place, eyes bulging, when they saw the hissing dynamite sticks coming toward them, flipping end over end. The one at the front wall found his legs first and began to scramble backward, but the other two were just barely in motion when the deadly dynamite reached the roof. Suddenly the air was split by a rapid series of thunderous concussions as the dynamite exploded.

Two of the riflemen on the roof were killed instantly, while the others were only knocked off their feet. Then a second batch of dynamite was tossed, and the last of the riflemen met their deaths, one by decapitation. The explosion sent some of the female dogs racing off.

On the ground, the guerrillas were having an even harder time keeping their dogs under control as the animals yelped in fear and strained at their leashes. Recovering from the shock of the first explosions, the Guatemalans whipped their heads around and looked up to see what had happened. Then one of the guerrillas shouted to his comrades and pointed at the north wall—and at the men who were scrambling over it, guns blazing. Leveling their rifles, the guerrillas released the frenzied dogs and immediately began to fight back.

Trinidad Cardenas and the other Mexicans in the wagon kept their eyes on the roof, ready to take out riflemen who might have survived the explosions. When a full minute had passed without sight of any, they grabbed guns from the wagon and went to join the fight.

Stepping inside the mansion, U.S. Marshal John McCain followed José Gristo down the vestibule, their heels clicking on the shiny marble floor. They passed through a pair of double doors into a vast room where the only furnishing was a large crystal chandelier hanging from the high ceiling. Directly ahead of them was a wide, winding staircase that led to the second floor. Off to the right was a pair of closed doors, behind which, McCain assumed, was a den or possibly a library. Juan Jaramillo had said the Campbells were being held in the second bedroom from the front of the house on the south side. Gristo was heading for that very hallway.

The dogs outside began to bark loudly, and Gristo abruptly stopped and looked back past McCain, who stopped as well. The marshal waited for the guerrilla to turn and continue on, but the swarthy man—apparently realizing that something was going on—suddenly reached for the gun on his hip, commanding, "You are going no farther, *señor!*"

Instinct and reflex developed from years as a lawman saved John McCain's life. Reacting instantly, he kicked Gristo in the groin with all his might, and the Guatemalan grunted and doubled over in agony. The muscular McCain then chopped him hard with a blow to the temple, and Gristo went down, the gun slipping from his fingers.

McCain heard male voices coming from a room somewhere down the hall. There was an open door off the hall to the right about forty feet away and two closed doors in between. McCain decided to drag Gristo to the room with the open door before other guerrillas put in an appearance and found he had assaulted their leader. The commotion the Dobermans were making outside increased, and the marshal saw in his mind Trinidad Cardenas pulling the wagon to a halt in front of the mansion. That meant Ray Gonzales and his mounted men were waiting at the edge of the forest to charge in for the battle.

As McCain leaned over to grasp the guerrilla leader, Gristo regained consciousness and clawed for McCain's gun. The marshal batted his hand aside and then banged him savagely on the nose. Gristo fell over backward, and McCain was on him quickly, pounding his face. But the Guatemalan fought back gamely, clearly determined to best his opponent, and he lashed out at the lawman with powerful fists. They traded blows three times, and then McCain threw a vicious uppercut, snapping back Gristo's head. He bounced off the wall and staggered near the open door off the north side of the hall. McCain went after him.

At that moment three rapid explosions boomed above the house, and gunfire erupted outside. A door farther down the hall opened, and two guerrillas came charging out of the room, guns in hand. When they saw McCain fighting their leader, they raised their weapons and fired. But the federal man anticipated their move in time to sink his fingers into Gristo's shirt and spin him toward the two guerrillas. Both bullets ripped into Gristo's back, killing him.

Suddenly from a room toward the front of the hallway another door opened, and several more guerrillas appeared, guns ready for action. They immediately spread out in the hall, bringing their revolvers to bear on the lawman. Thinking fast, McCain dropped Gristo and dived through the open door a step away.

But the Guatemalans at both ends of the hall had already lined their weapons on the stranger, and they fired. Two of them traded bullets, killing each other. The others swore and headed for the door through which McCain had just disappeared.

Dynamite explosions rocked the house again as the first guerrilla stepped through the doorway. McCain was flattened against the wall beside the door with his cocked gun ready. The revolver roared, and the .45 caliber slug tore clear through the man's head. Instinctively, McCain dropped to the floor next to the wall, ready to fire again, as the others came through the door with guns blazing, shooting wildly from waist level in a desperate attempt to take the intruder down. From his prone position, John McCain blasted each man. One of them was killed instantly, but the other, although felled by the slugs, was able to hold onto his gun. Staggering to his feet, he moved toward McCain, bringing his weapon up. The marshal fired again, drilling him in the heart, and the guerrilla stumbled through the doorway and fell flat in the hallway.

McCain leapt up and stepped into the hall, looking in both directions. Four corpses lay on the floor, but no one else was in sight. Knowing he must get to the Campbells quickly, he dashed up the hall and pounded on the second door on the south side, shouting, "Secretary Campbell! I am U.S. Marshal John McCain! The fighting you hear outside is a rescue team here to free you! Let me in!"

When there was no response, McCain tried the knob and was surprised when the door came open. Bolting inside, he could see that the room had been occupied— but now it was empty. He swore heatedly. While thinking about where the prisoners might be, McCain looked down at the gun in his hand and realized he did not remember how many shots he had fired. Quickly he broke it open and found that all six shells had been fired. Spilling the empty cartridges on the floor, he moved back into the hall, his mind fixed on one thing: He had to find the Campbells.

Just as McCain stepped into the hall and was reaching for his cartridge belt for live ammunition, the back door of the mansion flew open, and one of the guards entered with a leashed Doberman. Over the noise of battle outside, the swarthy man pointed at the intruder and, un-hooking the leash, screamed at the dog, "Get him!"

The Doberman charged toward the stranger, fangs bared. McCain felt a pang of helplessness, holding an empty gun while the vicious beast streaked at him full speed, bounding over the dead bodies. In what seemed a split second, the black dog was airborne, aiming its sharp teeth at John McCain's throat. Timing his move perfectly, he sidestepped the animal, and it sailed past him. The dog hit the floor, slid several yards along the smooth marble and then righted itself, pivoted, and sprang at McCain, a deep growl coming from its chest.

The guerrilla was moving slowly up the hallway, holding his gun at the ready, but he did not shoot, apparently for fear of hitting the dog.

Drops of spittle sprayed from the Doberman's mouth as it came snapping and snarling again. McCain dodged it once more, but this time he dropped his empty gun and seized the animal by the scruff of the neck with one hand and just above the rump with the other. The Doberman twisted its head violently back and forth, trying to bite the hand that held it.

Coming fast, the guerrilla was waiting for a clear shot at the intruder, and McCain suddenly ran toward him, holding the dog in his powerful grip. The lawman then heaved the snarling dog at him, and man and animal went down in a heap. At the same time, McCain made a dive for the revolver that lay beside one of the men he had killed. Lying on his belly, he scooped up the gun and cocked the hammer.

The snarling Doberman was on its feet again, although slipping on the floor in its fury to attack McCain, and the guerrilla was getting to his knees and bringing his gun to bear. Seeking to eliminate the greater threat first, McCain fired and hit the guard square in the forehead. The man's head whipped back from the impact, and blood sprayed the wall. His body tumbled over backward and went limp.

The Doberman stepped over the body and raced wildly at McCain, its great jaws gaping. Pointing the muzzle at the ferocious beast, the lawman snapped back the hammer and pulled the trigger. The sound of the hammer slamming down on an empty cartridge seemed louder than the deafening bark of the oncoming dog. He had not figured on the guerrilla's gun being empty, too. As the flashing fangs reached him, McCain desperately jammed the empty gun into the wide-open mouth, smashing the animal's teeth.

Howling, the maddened animal intensified its effort to reach McCain's neck, snarling, snapping, and biting violently. Jagged, broken fangs tore at the marshal's right arm as he threw it in front of his face in an attempt to fend off the slashing attack. The gun slipped from his fingers and rattled to the floor, and when McCain reached for it, sharp teeth ripped at his face, breaking skin. Warm blood flowed instantly.

Swinging an elbow as hard as he could, McCain connected solidly on the dog's head and sent it rolling. He got to his knees and spotted the revolver that had fallen from the hand of the dog's handler. Before the Doberman could fully recover from the blow to its head, the marshal lunged for the gun, grasped it, and cocked the hammer while rolling over to meet the black beast as it sprang at him, mouth open wide.

Aiming the muzzle directly at the vicious gaping mouth, praying that it was loaded, John McCain fired. The gun bucked against his palm as it roared, sending the bullet past the gnashing teeth and blowing a hole the size of a man's fist in the back of the Doberman's head. The dog flipped over and lay still in the grip of death.

Gasping for breath, the marshal groped his way up the wall and leaned against it. The sleeve on his right forearm was in shreds and soaked with blood, and he could feel the blood dripping off his chin from the gash on his left cheek. Getting his wind for a few seconds, he then made his way up the hall toward his fallen gun.

McCain picked up his revolver and loaded it, all the while listening to the intense battle raging outside. Slipping the Colt .45 into its holster, he entered what had been the Campbells' room. He had to locate them as quickly as possible, but first he had to attend to his bleeding right forearm. Hurrying across the room to one of the beds, he threw back the covers and then tore off a length of sheet. There was a pitcher of water on a small table next to the bed, and he rolled back the shredded sleeve and poured water over his bleeding cuts, noting that both his hands were also covered with slashes—although, fortunately, they were not deep. He carefully wrapped the piece of sheet around the forearm and knotted it with his teeth.

Crossing to a large dresser, he looked into the attached mirror and examined the gash on his face. It did not seem too bad, and the blood was already clotting. It could wait. The most important thing at that moment was to find the Campbells. Drawing his revolver and cocking it in case another emergency arose, he started down the hall, entering every room. He would search the entire first floor, and if he did not find the Campbells, he would cover the rest of the house. They had to be somewhere near.

Outside the mansion, Ray Gonzales and his men were engaged in a fierce encounter with the guards. Men were shouting violent oaths, screaming with pain, and battling with all their might. Guns blazed and roared, cutting down Mexicans and Guatemalans alike.

When guns went empty, the combatants pulled knives, and the men locked in hand-to-hand combat. The dogs entered the fight, snarling, ripping, and tearing at the bold intruders.

As the battle outside raged, John McCain checked every room on the first floor of the mansion, but there was no sign of the Campbells. Having found a door to the cellar off the kitchen, he dashed down there, calling out as he groped his way amid the deep shadows, but there was no response. He searched the cellar thoroughly and then bounded back up the stairs to the main floor.

Worry scratched at the marshal's mind as he contemplated the only other alternative: The Campbells had to have been moved to the second floor. The dynamite had no doubt torn holes in the roof, and he wondered if he would find the people he had come to rescue injured—or even dead.

McCain was racing through the house to the winding staircase, taking the stairs two at a time, when he abruptly stopped. The sounds of conflict outside had ceased, he realized, and listening intently, he heard a low rumble of voices growing louder as men came closer to the front door of the mansion.

John McCain's heart leapt to his throat. He had felt confident that even though Ray Gonzales and his bunch were outnumbered, the element of surprise would give them an edge. Had they come out victorious . . . or had they all been killed by the guerrillas and the dogs? Was it friend or foe about to step through the door?

The marshal tensed as he heard the front door open. When he recognized Ray Gonzales's voice, he smiled, relaxed, and started back down the stairs.

The Mexicans came in with their weapons ready, first eyeing the bodies strewn down the hallway and then finding the tall U.S. marshal. Ray Gonzales gestured at the makeshift bandage on McCain's arm and hurried toward him, asking, "Are you all right?"

McCain assessed the group of Mexicans standing before him; they were as tattered and bloody as he. Smiling crookedly, he nodded and replied, "Yeah. I'm all right. How'd it go out there?"

Gonzales replied, "Six of my men are dead and two are seriously wounded, but we killed all the guards and dogs we encountered outside. There were some other guerrillas in here, no?"

"There were," McCain responded, without elaborating.

Gonzales and the rest of the men stepped to their left and looked down the hallway. Seeing all the bodies, the burly Mexican stared wide-eyed at McCain and asked in an astonished voice, "You did all of that by yourself? Even the dog?"

"Not exactly," the lawman answered wryly. "Two of them shot each other." Becoming serious, he added, "But we've got a problem. I've searched this floor and the cellar, and I can't find the Campbells."

Ray Gonzales's bushy eyebrows arched. "They were not in the room where they were supposed to be?"

"No. I was about to search the second floor when you came in. Let's get up there and see if we can find them."

Turning to a husky, muscular man, Gonzales instructed,

"Manuel, you stay here and keep watch while the rest of us go with the marshal. I don't think any of us exactly took the time to count. Who knows? There may be another guard lurking around somewhere."

The man nodded his agreement, and then John McCain led the others up the winding staircase. Reaching the landing, they all spread out, but within five minutes John McCain and the Mexicans met at the top of the staircase. Every room and closet had been searched, and the Campbells were nowhere to be found.

Ray Gonzales sighed and asked, "What do you think, Marshal?"

McCain shook his head and ran his fingers through his dark hair. "There's only one answer, Ray. They've taken the Campbells elsewhere."

"I hope they are not buried out back," Gonzales remarked dismally.

The lawman had started to reply when movement at the bottom of the winding staircase caught his attention. Looking down, he saw Manuel Ramos dragging one of the guerrillas across the marble floor from the long hallway. Gonzales and his men leaned over the railing to see what the lawman was staring at.

After easing the guerrilla's head down, Ramos looked up at McCain and with a wry smile told him, "You only killed some of those guerrillas, Marshal. This one is still alive."

McCain turned to Gonzales and exclaimed excitedly, "He can tell us where they've taken the Campbells!"

Bounding down the stairs, with the Mexicans trailing, McCain stood over the guerrilla and recognized him as the one he had shot and left for dead in the room midway down the hall. There were two bullet holes in his left side and his shirt was soaked with blood. His glassy eyes were open and he was breathing rapidly and shallowly. It was clear that he did not have long to live.

"You did not find the Campbells?" asked Ramos.

"No," replied McCain, kneeling down beside the mortally wounded Guatemalan. "They've moved them to some other place. But this fellow is going to tell us where they are."

Putting his face directly in front of the Guatemalan's, John McCain said to the wounded guerrilla, "Secretary Campbell and his family were taken from this house and hidden elsewhere. Tell me where they are."

Bloody foam bubbled from the guerrilla's mouth as he worked his jaw and said weakly, "The Campbells . . . were never . . . here."

McCain's lips pulled tight. "You're lying! They were seen being brought here! Now, out with it! Where are they?"

The guerrilla stared at him, but said nothing.

"Make it easy on yourself," McCain warned. "Tell me what I want to know."

Hate showed in the guerrilla's glassy eyes as he whispered hoarsely, "I will never tell you!"

Losing his patience, temper suddenly coursed through John McCain. Placing a fist between the man's two bullet holes, he pushed hard on the man's chest and shouted, "Where are they!"

The guerrilla screamed in agony, tossing his head back and forth.

McCain hissed, "If you want some more pain, I can deliver it!"

"No! No!" gasped the dying man. "I will tell you!"

"That's better," McCain rejoined. "Let's hear it."

Blood ran from the corner of the guerrilla's mouth as he said with effort, "Two of our . . . outside guards disappeared . . . a few days ago. When . . . when this happened, José Gristo . . . became suspicious."

"I'm listening."

"Then . . . then when two more of the guards disappeared a couple . . . of days later, José was certain something was going on, and he had the . . . Campbells moved to an old . . . an old farmhouse a few miles west of here."

"How many miles?" demanded McCain.

The guerrilla swallowed hard, coughed, and closed his eyes.

The marshal feared the man would die before he could give them the location of the farmhouse. "How many miles?" he repeated sternly.

The guerrilla coughed again, bringing more bloody foam to his lips. Obviously speaking with effort, he gasped, "Five . . . five miles. Due west. It is a . . . brown house and . . . outbuildings. Near a small water . . . water—" The guerrilla coughed again and let out his last breath. His head lolled to one side, and the life left his body.

John McCain stood up. Looking around at the Mexicans, he said in a low voice, "That ought to be enough. Five miles due west. Brown outbuildings near a waterfall. I'm sure that's what he was trying to say, a waterfall."

"*Sí*," agreed Gonzales. "That is enough. I will leave a couple of my men to take the wounded ones to the doctor, and the rest of us will go with you, Marshal. We will find the Campbells and rescue them." He smiled, clapping the lawman on the shoulder. "That is a promise, *mi amigo*."

Chapter Six

U.S. Marshal John McCain and the band of Mexicans went outside. Looking around, McCain counted up the dead guerrillas and noted that six were missing from the number given him by Juan Jaramillo. That could only mean the missing Guatemalans were holding the Campbells at the farmhouse.

Turning to Ray Gonzales, the lawman said, "Let's get going. Seven of you plus me makes eight. That ought to be enough to take out the six of them." As they started toward the road, the lawman suggested, "I'll drive the wagon Trinidad Cardenas used to haul the dogs in. We can bring the Campbells back in it."

"Fine," Gonzales agreed. "I noticed the Guatemalans have a wagon and horses in the barn. My men can hitch the team and use that wagon to take our wounded *compadres* into town."

Moments later, John McCain was seated on the wagon seat, and he snapped the reins smartly. The wagon bounded off down the road, with Ray Gonzales and his men following on horseback.

McCain drove the wagon at as fast a pace as he could. Finally he drew up to the top of a hill and below saw a cluster of brown buildings nestled among a stand of trees in a shallow valley. Pulling rein, the lawman halted the wagon, and he remarked to Gonzales when the Mexican drew alongside the vehicle, "I'd say this is mighty close to five miles, wouldn't you?"

"Sí," agreed the beefy fighter, his brown eyes taking in the area. "And I believe I can hear water flowing, but I cannot see it."

"Over there!" spoke up Manuel Ramos, pointing toward a small waterfall to the north of the brown buildings that was partially hidden by thick brush.

"This is the place, all right," McCain declared. Setting the brake on the wagon, he ordered, "We'll leave the wagon and your horses up here and go in on foot."

The men dismounted, and bending low and keeping to the thick brush that dotted the hillside, McCain led the rescue team to within forty yards of the old farmhouse, where they stopped and surveyed the area. Several horses were in the corral at the barn to the rear of the house, and saddles were draped over the top rail of the corral fence. Abruptly, two Guatemalans came walking around a corner of the house, carrying rifles.

"Patrol guards!" whispered Gonzales. Removing his sombrero and taking out his knife, he said, "Manuel and I will eliminate them. Come on, Manuel!"

Also removing his hat and pulling his knife, the husky Ramos grinned and remarked, "With pleasure!"

McCain and the others bellied down in the grass and peered through the brush as the two Mexicans worked their way closer to the house, keeping to the thicket.

The guerrillas were smoking cigarettes and chatting leisurely. They stopped and sat on a large tree stump and continued to carry on a casual conversation, and it was apparent that they were not expecting anyone to show up. After a few minutes, Gonzales and Ramos had crept almost behind the guards, and McCain was relieved that the spot where the guards had paused could not be seen from the house.

The Mexicans stealthily moved directly in back of the unsuspecting guerrillas. Suddenly, two muscular bodies sprang out of the shadows, each throwing an arm around his victim's neck and driving a knife into his heart. The Mexicans quickly dragged the corpses into the brush. Then they hurried back to where McCain and the others waited.

Reaching them, Ray Gonzales picked up his sombrero and put it on and then breathed, "Two down and four to go, Marshal."

"Good work!" commented McCain. "Okay, let's stay in the brush and circle around to the barn. Somehow we've got to draw the other four out of the house. I don't want to take any chances on getting the Campbells hurt."

Within minutes, the men were gathered behind the barn. McCain sent Antonio Barillo in close to see what he could find out. He returned moments later, saying he could hear the guerrillas talking on the enclosed back porch. He was sure there were four of them in the group.

"Did you see any sign of the Campbells?" asked the marshal.

"No," replied Barillo. "It is my guess they are inside the house."

"Probably tied up," put in Gonzales.

John McCain leaned against the barn, trying to think of a way to lure the guerrillas outside. Manuel Ramos was peering around the corner of the building, watching the house, when he suddenly waved a hand and whispered, "Hey! One of them just came out! I think he is headed for that privy over there!"

The privy was some thirty yards from the back of the house, behind what appeared to be an old toolshed—and the toolshed blocked any view of the privy from the house. Anxiously, John McCain and the others watched as the guerrilla came their way from the house and then turned and entered the privy.

"I'll get him!" whispered McCain.

Manuel Ramos looked at the blood-soaked piece of sheet on the marshal's arm and said, "Maybe you should not try it, Señor McCain. Let me take him!"

"Okay," McCain agreed, smiling. To all, he whispered, "I believe if we take this one, at least one more will come to see why he has not returned. Then another will come to see why *that* one has not returned. Three times . . . and it's all over!"

The Mexicans smiled broadly, nodding with delight.

Moments later, Manuel Ramos jumped the guerrilla as he stepped out of the privy, killing him quietly with a knife blade through the heart. So as not to leave heel marks by dragging the man, he threw him over his shoulders and carried him behind the barn, dumping the lifeless form on the ground. Then he took up his position behind the privy once again.

Breathlessly, the men waited. Nearly twenty minutes had passed when a second guerrilla appeared at the back door and called, "Leo! Hey, Leo! Did you fall asleep in there or something?"

There was laughter behind the man. He waited a moment and then shouted loudly again, "Leo! Can you hear me?"

When no answer came, a worried look came over the guerrilla's face. He turned, said something to those inside and then pulled the gun from his holster and started in the direction of the privy. Instantly, the other Guatemalans appeared, carrying rifles.

"Now we've got them all!" McCain whispered excitedly.

The Mexicans whipped out their guns, leaning toward the corner of the barn. The marshal waved a hand, signaling for them to stay put. "Let them get real close," he instructed softly, pulling his own gun. "When I start firing, all of you swing out there and let them have it! Remember, we can't let any of them escape!"

Tension mounted while McCain kept a steady watch around the corner of the barn.

When the three guerrillas passed the toolshed and drew up to the privy, John McCain stepped around the edge of the barn, gun ready. The lawman in him would not allow

him to gun his enemies down without at least letting them
see him before he started shooting. The Mexicans immediately fanned out beside him, and the guerrillas practically jumped with surprise when they saw them. The one
with the revolver swore and brought his gun into play,
and John McCain immediately fired, hitting him in the
chest. Gonzales and his men then blazed away, unleashing
a barrage of bullets on the other two.

It was quickly evident that the Guatemalans were dead,
and McCain started running for the house, keeping his
weapon in hand in case there had been a miscount. The
Mexicans followed, although Manuel Ramos paused briefly
to make certain that the guerrillas were no longer a threat.

His gun ready, the marshal moved up cautiously to the
door of the back porch and pulled it open. There was no
one in sight. Knowing the Campbells would be wondering
what had happened, he called out, "Secretary Campbell,
are you in there? My name is John McCain! United States
Marshal John McCain! I have some Mexicans with me,
and we just killed your captors!"

He heard both a quavering whimper and a woman
bursting into tears.

"Yes, Marshal!" called Duncan Campbell. "We're in the
parlor!"

McCain bolted across the porch, through the kitchen,
and into the parlor at the front of the house. Ray Gonzales
and his men were on his heels. Bursting into the room,
the lawman found the Campbells tied to chairs that had
been huddled together. The two women were facing him,
while Duncan Campbell was sitting with his back toward
McCain. Patricia Campbell, her head bowed and her di-
sheveled hair fallen over her face, was weeping with relief.

John McCain's gaze then fell on Lucy Campbell. There
were tears of relief in her eyes as well, but she gave the
lawman a ready smile—which immediately warmed his
heart. He smiled back as he walked over to her and told
her softly, "It's going to be all right now, Miss Campbell.

We'll soon have you sleeping in your own bed—which I imagine will feel like paradise at this point." Kneeling beside Lucy's chair, McCain looked over his shoulder and instructed the Mexicans to untie Patricia and Duncan Campbell while he freed the young woman from her bonds.

As McCain worked on Lucy's rope, he looked at the secretary and asked, "Are any of you hurt, sir?"

"No, although my wife is terribly exhausted—and frightened almost out of her mind," breathed Campbell. "Thank God you're here. How did you find us?"

"It's a long story, sir," replied the marshal. "We'll tell you all about it later. I'll say this much right now: We stormed the mansion and killed all the guerrillas who were there. Fortunately one of them lived long enough to tell us where you were."

The moment Lucy's hands came free, she stood and put her arms around her mother. "It's all over now. We're safe," she murmured comfortingly, almost as though their roles had been reversed.

When his ropes came loose, Duncan Campbell got to his feet, although he was somewhat unsteady as a result of being forced to sit bound in one spot for so long. Rubbing his wrists, he said, "Did I hear right? You're a United States marshal?"

"Yes, sir," the lawman confirmed, extending his hand. "John McCain."

As the war secretary shook McCain's hand he asked, "Who sent you to rescue us?"

"It was a direct order from President Cleveland, sir."

Smiling broadly, Campbell commented on the President's generous concern and then asked about the Mexicans who had aided McCain in the rescue. The marshal introduced Ray Gonzales and the others to Campbell, explaining that a number of Gonzales's men had given their lives or had been seriously wounded in the battle at the mansion. Deeply touched, the secretary of war expressed his profound appreciation to Gonzales.

Patricia Campbell got to her feet, assisted by her daughter. Wiping away her tears, she told McCain and the others, "There is no way we can thank all of you for doing this. We were beginning to give up hope that any help was coming."

Lucy brushed a fallen lock of blond hair from her face and gazed at the tall, handsome lawman. When their eyes met, McCain realized he had been staring at her, captivated by her stunning beauty.

"Marshal McCain," she said, "you and these men have done a very brave and unselfish thing." Her brow furrowed as she added, "Your battle must have been a fierce one. All of you have been bloodied."

Unable to stop staring at the young woman, McCain responded, "We'll be fine, miss. We're just glad we found you alive and well."

"What now, Marshal?" queried Campbell.

McCain could feel Lucy intently studying his face in return, and he practically had to force himself to look at the war secretary rather than at his daughter as he replied, "We know that there are other Guatemalan guerrillas in this part of the country, Mr. Campbell. We just don't know where they are. It'll be much safer if we wait until nightfall to take you and your family out of here. We have a hiding place all set up for you, and you'll remain there until the day after tomorrow, when you'll be transported back to Juárez by stagecoach. Once we get you across the Rio Grande into El Paso, we'll put you on the first train going east."

The war secretary expressed his skepticism about the use of a stagecoach, but when John McCain explained his reasons for doing so, Campbell understood and wholeheartedly agreed.

Ray Gonzales then said to McCain, "Marshal, I need to return to the mansion and pick up my dead for burial, and I also need to go into Chihuahua and check on the men who were wounded. I will leave Manuel, Antonio, and

Alonzo to escort you and the Campbells to Rondo's place, if that is acceptable. Since they will be going on the stagecoach with us, it will give these good people an opportunity to get acquainted with them."

"That's a good idea, Ray," McCain agreed.

As soon as Gonzales had left, Lucy looked at John McCain and said, "Marshal, that gash on your cheek should be cleaned, and perhaps a fresh bandage for your arm would be in order."

The attention given him by the beautiful blonde sent a tingle down U.S. Marshal John McCain's spine. Trying not to be too obvious, he studied her face, admiring the natural luscious red of her lips and the extraordinary blue of her eyes. Aside from her beauty, she was showing amazing poise, and McCain thought she had held up surprisingly well under the rigors of captivity. This Lucy Campbell was a remarkable young woman . . . and McCain found himself having the fleeting thought that she would make a good wife for a lawman.

While her father was fetching water from a well outside, Lucy found a bed sheet. Sitting the marshal down on a chair in the kitchen, she removed the bloody bandage from his right forearm and washed the wound thoroughly. John McCain was enjoying her closeness.

When she had replaced the bandage on his arm, she examined the wound on his face. "What made this awful gash?" she asked, her voice filled with concern.

"Well, I ran into one of the Dobermans face to face . . . literally."

Lucy shuddered. "You're lucky you weren't hurt any worse than you were."

He grinned crookedly. "You're right."

Dipping a clean, wadded cloth in cool water, she leaned close and dabbed tenderly at the wound. Her warm breath touched McCain's face and set his heart pounding so hard, he could hear it inside his head. He marveled that Lucy did not hear it.

After a few moments, she told him, "That's the best I can do, Marshal. Maybe you should have a doctor look at it when you get back to town. He might want to take a few stitches."

"I'll consider your advice, Miss Campbell. And I thank you for your help," the enamoured lawman replied, thinking how much he would like to give her a kiss in payment for her medical services. Quickly he reprimanded himself, reminding himself that John McCain was a mere federal lawman, while Lucy Campbell was the daughter of a high official in the President's cabinet. They lived in two vastly different worlds. And besides, the mere fact that in the few moments he had known her he had found her the most remarkable and beautiful woman he had ever met did not mean that she felt anything special toward him. *I'm being an utter fool!* he told himself sharply. *Quit acting like a schoolboy and get down to business, McCain!*

When darkness finally fell, the exhausted group headed across the rugged land toward Rondo Ortega's place. The group arrived about an hour and a half later, having made the trip to the barn without incident. They were delighted to find that Ray Gonzales had taken time to stop and inform Rondo of the situation, and their host had a sumptuous meal prepared for them.

Soon after eating, the weary prisoners and John McCain fell gratefully onto the cots in Ortega's hidden cellar. Within minutes, the rescued and the rescuer were sound asleep.

The brilliant sun shone from a flawless sky a half hour before noon on May 19, 1893, as U.S. Marshal John McCain loaded a small box of dynamite into the brightly colored stagecoach behind the Alegre Viaje Stage Line office. Rubin Lupino was backing the six-up team into place, preparing to hitch them to the coach. Julio Herrera stood on the back porch of the office, keeping a proprietary eye on everything.

McCain stepped into the barn for a few moments and then returned carrying four rifles and four revolvers, along with a cloth sack bearing several boxes of cartridges. As he placed them inside the coach, Herrera walked over to him and commented, "You certainly are traveling well armed, Señor McCain."

"These are all extras," replied the marshal. "I figure we can't be too careful. If we have to fight more Guatemalan guerrillas, I don't want to be short on firepower."

At that moment, Ray Gonzales, Manuel Ramos, Antonio Barillo, and Alonzo Montoya rode into the yard. Gonzales eyed the lawman and asked, "How is the arm, Señor McCain?"

"Doing fine, thank you," McCain assured him.

"It should," spoke up Manuel Ramos with a sly grin on his face.

"Meaning?" McCain queried.

Ramos chuckled. "Meaning that I never saw a man enjoy getting doctored up as much as you were enjoying it."

The marshal's face reddened, and he was embarrassed that he had been so obvious. Nonetheless, he protested, "Now, just a minute!"

"Do not try to deny that you were lapping up her attention like a thirsty pup laps up cool water, Señor McCain!" cut in Montoya.

The Mexicans laughed heartily. Before the lawman could make any kind of rejoinder, they wheeled their horses around and headed to the corral, where they would leave their mounts during the journey. When they returned, John McCain showed them the arsenal aboard the stage, the dynamite, and the iron plates in the doors.

"I guess we are ready for trouble," commented Ray Gonzales.

"We are—but I sure hope it doesn't come," breathed McCain. With the stagecoach fully loaded, Rubin Lupino brought it around to the front of the office, where it would normally wait for embarking passengers.

He had no sooner finished breaking the coach to a halt when Rondo Ortega's wagon appeared, accompanied by five of Ray Gonzales's men on horseback. John McCain and the others met the wagon as it pulled up, and as soon as Herrera and Lupino had scanned the street to make sure no strangers were lurking about, they gave the word to McCain.

Looking into the wagon bed, McCain addressed the three people sitting there, their shoulders swathed in serapes and their faces concealed by large sombreros. "All right, folks," he told the Campbells. "You can board the stagecoach now."

Duncan Campbell hopped from the wagon and then helped his wife down. John McCain offered his hand to Lucy, who took it graciously, giving him a warm smile. Alighting, she looked up at the tall lawman, and when their eyes met, it seemed to McCain as though a current ran through him. He kept her hand in his, and when the moment began to stretch too long, Lucy cleared her throat softly and said, "Thank you, Marshal."

"My pleasure," he responded.

The blonde seemed to be having as much trouble disengaging from the lawman as he from her. Finally she pulled her eyes from McCain's and focused instead on the stagecoach. Gesturing at the lettering above the door, she said, "Alegre Viaje Stage Line. What does 'Alegre Viaje' mean, Marshal?"

"It means joyful journey, Miss Campbell," replied McCain.

"Well," she chirped with a smile, "I certainly hope this turns out to be a joyful journey!"

John McCain did not comment. It was a long way to Juárez, and he had developed a healthy respect for the toughness and the resourcefulness of the Guatemalan guerrillas. He could only hope they did not learn that the Campbells were being transported by the stage.

Antonio Barillo walked slowly past the six-up team,

looking them over, and then climbed up into the box. Looking down at McCain, he said, "It's high noon, Señor McCain. Time for us to go."

"So it is," McCain replied. "Okay, everybody. Let's get loaded."

The Campbells thanked Rondo Ortega and their escorts and then entered the coach. Ray Gonzales and Manuel Ramos climbed in next, leaving the seat directly across from the beautiful blonde for U.S. Marshal John McCain. McCain caught their eyes and surreptitiously smiled. Finally Alonzo Montoya, wearing two revolvers and carrying a twelve-gauge double-barreled shotgun and a .44 caliber Winchester seven-shot repeater, climbed up beside Antonio Barillo.

Turning to Rubin Lupino and Julio Herrera, McCain bid them farewell and then turned and started to enter the coach. Suddenly, Herrera laid a hand on McCain's shoulder and said urgently, "Marshal—wait a minute!"

McCain pivoted and followed the agent's gaze across the street, but with so many pedestrians, riders, and vehicles moving about, the marshal could not tell what Herrera was looking at. "What is it?" he asked.

Pointing with his chin, Herrera said, "Those four riders in front of the cantina, they are not from this town. They rode in and stopped over there a few minutes ago, but they still have not dismounted, and they keep looking over here at the stagecoach."

John McCain felt a coldness settle in his stomach. Glancing inside the coach, he saw the Campbells watching him with worried expressions on their faces. He looked back at the cantina and found the four swarthy riders looking directly back at him. "Do you think they could be Guatemalans?" he quietly asked Herrera.

"Quite possibly," the agent responded, nodding.

Before McCain could say anything further, the men dismounted, still looking toward the coach.

McCain leaned inside and told the others, "Only thing to do is go talk to them."

"We'll go with you," Ray Gonzales insisted, stepping out of the coach, and Manuel Ramos followed. Gonzales then spoke to his men on horseback, telling them to dismount. Commanding a couple of them to stay with the Campbells, Gonzales told the rest of them to follow, and he and John McCain started across the street.

Assessing the band of men, McCain noted that each of them wore a sidearm and a large knife. As the lawman and the Mexicans drew up to the foursome, the strangers stiffened, but waited for the others to speak.

McCain ran his gaze over their faces and asked in Spanish, "Where are you men from?"

Bristling visibly, the largest of the men clenched his jaw and replied tartly, "What business is it of yours, *gringo*?"

"I'm making it my business because you seem to have an unusual interest in what's going on over there at the stage office."

"We were just admiring the stagecoach," the man said defensively. "That is all."

Ray Gonzales then said to the man, "I would be obliged if you would tell me your name and where you are from."

The man's prominent cheeks flushed angrily. "Since it is you who have approached me, I would think that you are obligated to tell me your identity first."

Ray Gonzales squared his muscular shoulders. "That is fair enough," he said, hooking his thumbs in his gun belt. "My name is Raimundo Luis Cristóbal Gonzales, and I am from the mountains a few miles west of here."

"And my name is Francisco Voliva," said the stranger. "I am from a town in the mountains *many* miles west of here—as are my friends."

"And what town is that?" demanded Gonzales.

Voliva's face darkened. "I think you have asked enough questions, Señor Gonzales. Unless you are with the *policía*, I will not answer any more."

Gonzales stepped so close to Voliva that his nose was no more than an inch from his. His black eyes riveted the man as he spoke in a gravelly voice. "It would be wise of you to weigh the situation, *señor*. There are twice as many of us as there are you. We have other business we wish to look after, and you are wearing our patience rather thin. The reasons for this interrogation are simple: You are strangers in Chihuahua, and at this particular time, strangers bother us . . . especially those who show unusual interest in our stagecoaches. Now, you will answer my questions, or we will beat all of you to bloody pulps. Do I make myself clear?"

Francisco Voliva glanced at his companions and then let a slow smile build on his lips. "You are very convincing in your argument, *señor*. We are from La Junta, a small town in the mountains some seventy-five miles west of here. You know of it?"

Relaxing his hot glare, Ray Gonzales eased back a step and replied, "*Sí*. I have been there many times. If you are telling me the truth, you will know the name of the mayor."

"His name is Alberto Gallegos."

Gonzales looked over his shoulder at McCain and said, "He is correct."

The marshal was not yet satisfied. It would not be hard for Guatemalans to know that. "Ask him something harder," he instructed Gonzales.

Looking Voliva in the eye again, Gonzales asked, "How long have you lived in La Junta?"

"All my life, and I am forty-two years old."

"Then you will know the name of the woman who was murdered in your town in January of eighteen seventy-four. Two men hanged her from the roof of a barn."

"*Sí*, the woman was Lolita Conchez, the wife of La Junta's schoolmaster."

Looking back at McCain, Gonzales said, "No Guatemalan could know that, Marshal. He is correct."

Relieved that the four strangers were not guerrillas, John McCain apologized for disturbing them and returned to the stage. There was a sigh of relief among the Campbells as well when McCain reported to them that everything was all right. The lawman and the Mexicans then boarded the stagecoach, and the vehicle finally rolled down the street and out of Chihuahua, heading northward.

Settling back in her seat, Lucy looked across at the marshal. It was evident that she was trying to disguise the fear in her voice when she asked, "Just what are our chances of making it to Juárez without being caught by the Guatemalan guerrillas, Marshal?"

McCain saw the trepidation in Lucy's eyes. "That's a hard question to answer, Miss Campbell. There's no way for us to know how soon the guerrillas will find out about your escape. But even when they do, I think there's a real good chance that they'll never figure on us transporting you to Juárez by stagecoach."

He flicked a glance at Patricia Campbell, who was showing genuine terror. Leaning toward her, he assured the woman, "The men on this stage have been chosen for a very good reason: They're the best fighting men in all of Mexico." He smiled, adding, "And I have more than a little experience at fighting myself. Believe me . . . we will do everything we can to get you safely to El Paso. We're staking our lives on it."

Chapter Seven

Up in the box of the stagecoach, Antonio Barillo kept the horses moving in a steady rhythm. Glancing to his right at his shotgunner, he said to Alonzo Montoya, "Remember what Ray instructed us: Do not let your guard down for a second."

"You do not have to worry about that," Montoya responded, gripping his rifle. "My eyes will be peeled all the way to Juárez."

Inside the coach, the Campbells were seated together on the front-facing seat, with their escorts facing them. Manuel Ramos was opposite Duncan Campbell on the starboard side, Ray Gonzales faced Patricia Campbell, and John McCain was exactly where he wanted to be—opposite beautiful Lucy Campbell.

Forcing himself to tear his eyes away from the blonde's captivating face, McCain looked over at the war secretary and said, "I've hardly had a chance to talk to you since we met, sir. What with getting things ready for this trip, I wasn't able to spend any time at Rondo's barn with you yesterday. Were you able to get things cleared up between our country and Mexico, Mr. Campbell?"

"Yes," replied Campbell, watching steadily out the window. "Everything's, uh, fine, now."

Wanting to be sociable and show interest in the secretary's work, McCain proceeded, "I suppose there were

97

more problems involved than just that takeover of the
Alamo by those Mexicans."

Campbell adjusted himself on the seat, met McCain's
gaze, and said, "Yes. There had been other things causing
conflict between their people and ours. That was just the,
uh, straw that broke the camel's back." The secretary's
gaze drifted out the window again.

It was clear that Duncan Campbell was reluctant to talk
further. McCain understood that the secretary was preoccupied, since he and his family had just been through a
terrible ordeal—and there was plenty of potential danger
ahead.

Silence prevailed in the coach. Then Lucy spoke up to
fill the awkward void. Smiling sweetly at McCain, she
asked, "Marshal, since none of us Campbells feels much
like talking, why don't you tell us something about yourself? I'd love to know where you're from, what made you
decide to become a lawman, and how long you've been a
federal marshal."

Pushing his hat to the back of his head, exposing his
thick head of dark, wavy hair, McCain replied, "I don't
want to bore you, Miss Campbell."

"Oh, it won't bore me," Lucy assured him, her eyes
shining brightly with eagerness.

Reluctant at first to talk about himself, the handsome
John McCain obliged. After some ten minutes of covering
his past and answering her questions, McCain guided the
conversation toward Lucy and her own background. Soon
they were engaged in enjoyable conversation, and before
they knew it, the stage was pulling into the first swing
station, some twelve miles from Chihuahua.

The stage rolled to a halt about fifty feet from the porch
of a flat-roofed adobe building that bore two signs, one
announcing that the building was a trading post and the
other, smaller, sign advertising that the building served as
an office for the Alegre Viaje Stage Line. There was a
small barn out back, partially surrounded by a corral.

Inside the corral were a dozen horses, all bred for hauling stagecoaches.

When John McCain stepped out of the coach and gave his hand to Lucy Campbell, he noticed several people loitering around the area, including a number of unsavory-looking young men. His body automatically tensed, prepared for a dangerous encounter, but he covered his apprehension, not wanting to alarm the Campbells.

The wind was picking up, and clouds were building from the north so quickly that they would soon cover the sun. Small dust devils were skipping about the place, throwing dirt and sand against the coach and the buildings. Alighting from the coach, Duncan Campbell looked at the sky and remarked to McCain, "Looks like we might be in for a storm."

"Could be," the marshal responded offhandedly, all the while watching the loiterers milling about. He recalled that when his coach had stopped at this same swing stop on the trip down, the same kind of crowd had been there . . . but this time, he was on the alert for Guatemalans. Turning to Patricia and Lucy, he said, "Ladies, there are privies out back. Just go through the trading post. They have water inside for you to drink, too."

Duncan Campbell guided his wife and daughter into the squat building as the agent came out and greeted Barillo and Montoya, asking if they had just hired on. Barillo told him they were only filling in for the regular driver and shotgunner.

While the horses were being changed, Barillo, Montoya, Ramos, and Gonzales also entered the trading post. John McCain acted as if he was interested in the work of the man who was changing horses, but he was actually surveying the faces of the men who were hanging around the station building.

Shortly, Ray Gonzales walked back to the stagecoach and stood beside McCain, following the lawman's wary eyes as they scanned different groups of men. Stepping close and speaking softly, Gonzales asked, "Are you thinking that some of those men could be Guatemalans, *amigo*?"

"That's exactly what I'm thinking," responded the marshal. "Trouble is, there's no way to be sure. Those guerrillas are a sharp bunch, and they'll do everything they can to blend into their surroundings so as to be inconspicuous. If they aren't mixing with Mexicans to hide themselves at this way station, they could be at one up the line. And we've got a long way to go."

Appearing as casual as the marshal, Gonzales studied the loiterers and then said from the side of his mouth, "All of them are wearing sidearms except for those three old men over there on the edge of the porch."

"I noticed that," said McCain.

"If some of them are Guatemalans, I do not know if they will be brazen enough to make their move right here or not. They might wait and follow the stage until there are no witnesses, then jump us."

McCain and Gonzales discussed the situation, although their attention was drawn to Antonio Barillo when he returned as he pitched in to help the agent finish hitching up the fresh team.

Moments later, Duncan Campbell came out of the station building with his wife and daughter, Alonzo Montoya, and rough-looking Manuel Ramos. They waited until the team had been hitched and then started off the porch, but as they did so, six young men surrounded them, forcing the travelers to stop.

Ignoring the dust swirling around him, Montoya glared at the youth directly in front of him and said, "Move. We need to board the stage."

When the man did not comply, Patricia Campbell's face twisted with fear and she grasped her husband's arm. But the man only had eyes for Lucy, and he was leering at her with a wanton smile on his lips. Lucy stiffened and shot a glance toward John McCain, but the marshal was deep in conversation with Ray Gonzales at the stagecoach.

The lecherous youth, who was clearly the gang's leader, began talking to Lucy, making suggestive remarks. Duncan Campbell's face purpled, and he blared, "Get away from my daughter!"

The young man disregarded him as if he had not spoken. Ramos and Montoya bristled, and Montoya growled, "Go about your business, and leave us to ours! Especially leave the *señorita* alone. She is not interested in the likes of you."

The ribald youths laughed boisterously, making it clear they were not above starting trouble.

Manuel Ramos stared hard at the leader, looking even fiercer than usual. "I am warning you. Take your friends and go on about your business."

"But pretty *señoritas* are my business!" the youth retorted contemptuously, clearly feeling he was safe, having the travelers outnumbered.

Montoya and Ramos looked at each other, obviously not sure what to do.

While the young man's friends looked on, laughing insolently, he reached out and ran his fingers through Lucy's long blond hair. "So soft and silky," he breathed hotly.

Lucy's eyes flashed with anger as she reached out and slapped his hand away. But her move served only to bring more laughter.

Duncan Campbell's face went livid with rage. He stepped between Lucy and the young man and roared, "You touch my daughter again, scum, and I'll break your filthy neck!"

Hearing Duncan Campbell's outburst, John McCain and Ray Gonzales looked over. When they realized what was going on, they were immediately in motion, and McCain told the Mexican as they strode quickly across the yard, "I'll take care of the big shot, Ray. You keep an eye on his pals."

Stepping alongside the Campbells, McCain looked down at the crude young Mexican. The lawman gave Lucy a reassuring look, asking, "What did he do to you, Miss Campbell?"

"He's been nasty and rude, and he put his hand in my hair."

McCain's eyes hardened as he snarled at the youth, "You had no right to lay a hand on her! We didn't come here looking for trouble, and I'd be willing to forget this whole incident when you apologize."

The impertinent Mexican laughed derisively and then turned to his friends, asking, "Did you hear that, *compañeros*? This dog-faced *gringo* is telling Felix Yorres he is going to make an apology to the *señorita!*"

Yorres's friends burst out laughing, and he shoved McCain back, reaching again for Lucy. Before Yorres could touch the young woman, McCain grabbed him and threw him to the ground, disarming him and ramming his face violently in the dirt. To his obvious surprise, Felix Yorres was pinned to the ground on his back under the weight of U.S. Marshal John McCain.

Alonzo Montoya suddenly bolted for the stagecoach, while Duncan Campbell put his arms protectively around his wife and daughter. One of the other youths swore and drew his revolver, but Manuel Ramos leapt at him, grasping the wrist that held the gun. The stout-bodied Ramos wrestled with the youth over control of the gun, meeting him strength for strength. Suddenly the gun went off, but fortunately it was pointed skyward.

Ramos shook the youth's wrist in an attempt to dislodge the revolver, but his opponent stubbornly held on as the wrestling match continued. The rest of Yorres's friends shot glances at each other, clearly trying to decide if they should get into the conflict.

They apparently made up their minds, for their hands dropped for their revolvers—but they went no further. Alonzo Montoya rushed in and pointed his shotgun at the foursome and bawled, "Do not try it!" Both hammers were cocked, and the youths froze. Gesturing with the black muzzles of the double-barreled shotgun, he added, "Let us see how quickly you fellows can drop those guns in the dirt."

Reluctantly, they obeyed.

Waving the shotgun menacingly, Montoya snapped, "Now the knives!"

Faces rigid and full of hate, the youths carefully pulled their knives from the leather sheaths on their belts and let them fall at their feet. Antonio Barillo, who was standing near, picked them up.

The obdurate youth, wrestling with Manuel Ramos, continued fighting for all he was worth. He swore at Ramos, grinding his teeth and saying, "I will kill you, swine! I will kill you!"

The expression on Ramos's face declared that he had had enough, and he abruptly brought a knee up savagely into his opponent's groin. The youth howled and doubled over. Jerking the gun from his hand, Ramos tossed it toward Barillo and then punched the hurting youth with a right and a left, rocking him on his heels. Ramos finished him off with a powerful blow to the jaw, and he collapsed in a heap.

John McCain lifted Felix Yorres to his feet. Gripping a fistful of shirt, McCain shook him violently, snapping his head back and forth. "Now Señor Felix Yorres, you are going to make an apology to this young woman for your rudeness!"

Yorres's face displayed contempt and impudence. Without warning, he spit a stringy blob of spittle onto the bridge of McCain's nose. Fury welled up in the lawman, and he lashed out with a fist and smashed the source of the spittle, splitting both of the Mexican's lips. He continued punching him again and again, and Yorres wailed loudly, spraying blood.

The Mexican's face was a mass of crimson when John McCain was finally satisfied that Felix Yorres was sufficiently punished. Holding him erect by the shirt, McCain told him slowly, deliberately, and coldly, "There are two things you are going to do now, Yorres. First, you are going to wipe the spittle from my face with one of your sleeves. Secondly, you are going to apologize to the young woman for your rudeness."

With a shaking hand, Felix Yorres performed the first of his tasks. Then he stumbled over to Lucy Campbell—propelled by the marshal's hand on the back of his neck. Blood was running from his obviously broken nose and from his mouth, turning the dirt on his face into reddened mud.

Facing the beautiful young woman, Yorres licked his lips and said quietly, "I . . . I apologize, *señorita.*"

Gritting his teeth and shaking him, McCain insisted, "Tell her what you apologize for!"

"I apologize for being rude to you."

"Is that all?" pressed McCain.

"What else is there?" snapped Yorres.

McCain jerked the Mexican's shirt collar, whipping his head. "You put your filthy hands on her, didn't you?"

Yorres turned and looked at the marshal. There was murder in his eyes—and McCain read it clearly. "Well, didn't you?" the lawman pressed.

"*Sí.*"

"Then tell her you are sorry for putting your filthy hands on her!"

Staring at the marshal with blazing eyes, Yorres bared his bloodstained teeth. The youth's obstinance infuriated McCain, and he shook him violently, whipping his head back and forth. "You do what I tell you, or so help me, I'll rearrange your face so that your own mother wouldn't know you! Now say it!"

It was apparent that Felix Yorres was in great pain—and it was equally apparent that he opted for an apology over further punishment. He finally choked out, "I . . . I am sorry I put my hands on you."

McCain shook him again. "You left out a word, bucko!

Say it again, and this time get it right. My patience is running thin."

Yorres glared at McCain again and then looked at Lucy and mumbled, "I am sorry I put my filthy hands on you."

"That's better," breathed the marshal, and flung Yorres to the dusty ground.

The youth rolled over and looked up at his conqueror, but he did not say anything.

Walking over to the Campbells, the marshal smiled at them and announced, "Time to get the stage moving, folks." Then, offering Lucy his arm, he asked, "May I escort you to your chariot, miss?"

As McCain and the Campbells headed to the stagecoach, the marshal called over his shoulder, "Ray, collect our friends' guns. We'll drop them on the road a mile or so from here."

The crowd stood still and the Mexican toughs looked on in anger as Ray Gonzales, backed up by Alonzo Montoya's shotgun, gathered up their guns. The men then walked swiftly toward the stage.

The rain was beginning to fall as the passengers boarded the coach and Antonio Barillo climbed up in the box to once again take the reins in hand. Alonzo Montoya stepped to the side of the coach, eased the hammers down on the shotgun, and climbed up beside Barillo.

The last to board was John McCain. Putting one foot inside, the lawman turned and stared unwaveringly at Felix Yorres, who was being helped to his feet by his friends. McCain held his gaze on the whipped youth for a long moment and then stepped in and closed the door. Barillo flicked the reins, shouted, "Heeyah!" and the stage moved out. As they rolled away from the swing station, the lawman gave a last look back. Felix Yorres stood shaking his fist angrily at the stagecoach, a look of murderous hatred on his bloodied face.

Overhead, huge black thunderheads swirled angrily, and to the north, distant rumbles of thunder heralded the coming storm. The wind began pelting the rain against the rolling coach, sending spray through the windows, and the leather curtains were quickly rolled down. Up in the box, Montoya and Barillo broke out the slickers that were kept in a metal container under the seat.

Everyone rode in silence, clearly thinking about the encounter. Finally Lucy Campbell smiled at Ray Gonzales and Manuel Ramos, telling them, "Thank you for coming to my rescue."

The two Mexicans grinned and mumbled, *"De nada."*

Catching the lawman's eye, she looked at him with a mixture of gratitude and delight and murmured, "You were wonderful, Marshal McCain. I can't tell you how grateful I am."

Staring at the beautiful young woman opposite him, John McCain found himself speechless for one of the few times in his life. After what seemed an interminable pause, he cleared his throat and responded, "It was my pleasure, Miss Campbell."

They looked into each other's eyes for a long moment, and then each looked away, slightly embarrassed by the intensity.

In less than a half hour, the stage was climbing into the Sierra del Nido range, and the higher they climbed, the harder it poured, until rain was coming down in torrents. Though it was only midafternoon, the heavy clouds made it so dark, it almost seemed like dusk. The mountain road was rough and steep, and the stage was bouncing unmercifully. Inside, the passengers were attempting to roll with the bumps, and the rear-facing men were bracing their feet on the slanting floor to keep from sliding off the seat and onto the Campbells' laps.

Up in the box, Barillo and Montoya bent their heads against the wind-driven rain, and Barillo had to crack his whip over the heads of the horses repeatedly to keep them moving at a steady pace. The thunder and lightning made the animals nervous, and the driving rain fought them every step of the way.

Shouting above the weather's din, Montoya said, "Where do we stop next, Antonio?"

"We are supposed to spend the night in a town called El Sauz!" Barillo shouted back, cracking the whip once more. "But I am wondering if we will get there before dark! We are not making very good progress!"

Montoya looked at his partner and said loudly, "Then we will have to go faster! We definitely do not want to be caught on this treacherous, muddy road after darkness falls! One slip in the dark, and we could go tumbling over the edge!"

Antonio Barillo nodded and swallowed hard. Cracking the whip over the horses' heads again, he cajoled them on toward El Sauz.

Chapter Eight

After reaching the top of an incline, the Alegre Viaje stagecoach started down the long, steep slope with wind and rain lashing it furiously. With the stage now slanting the other way, it was the Campbells who were bracing their feet on the floor to keep from sliding off their seats. Then the coach, which had been slowly descending the steep road for about five minutes, came to a halt at a sharply pitched angle.

All conversation between the passengers broke off, and U.S. Marshal John McCain pulled back the leather curtain on the window beside him and stuck his head out. Rain beat him in the face, but blinking against it, he shouted, "Antonio! Why have we stopped?"

Barillo called loudly from the box, "I hate to ask you to come out in the rain, Marshal, but you'd better take a look at this!"

McCain tightened his hat on his head, opened the door, and stepped out. Immediately McCain could distinguish a loud roar coming from somewhere below them. Barillo and Montoya waited alongside the coach as the lawman stepped to the ground and closed the door. Gesturing, Barillo said, "Come here, Marshal."

McCain felt the rain soaking through his clothing instantly as the driver led him a few yards forward, past the nervous team. Then Barillo stopped and pointed straight ahead. Forty feet in front of them was a raging river that, judging by the size of its bed, was normally just a good-sized creek. Now, swollen by the heavy rain, it was boiling furiously and was about to overflow its banks. The sound of the tumbling, plunging water was almost deafening.

Lightning lit the murky sky, followed by a cannonlike burst of thunder. Shouting above the noise, Antonio Barillo looked at John McCain and said, "There is no way we can cross it!"

"That's for sure!" agreed McCain. Scanning the area, he saw that there was a sheer wall of granite on one side, while on the other was a precipitous drop. The foaming river bottomed out directly in front of them, and if it flooded over its banks and rose much higher, they would be trapped. Pivoting to survey the incline behind them, he saw that Manuel Ramos, Ray Gonzales, and Duncan Campbell had left the coach and were slipping and sliding toward them, heads slanted against the driving curtain of rain.

As the trio drew up, they saw the thundering current below. Worry was evident on the war secretary's face as he looked at John McCain and shouted, "Marshal, what are we going to do?"

Before answering, the lawman gazed back up the steep road they had just traveled. It was slick with muddy water, and small stones were tumbling down its surface. Shaking his head, McCain lifted his voice and replied, "There's only one thing we *can* do! We've got to turn this rig around and get out of here! That stream is rising rapidly! When it overflows its banks, this area is going to be under water!"

"Then let's do it!" shouted Duncan Campbell, turning and heading back toward the stagecoach with the others. "I don't like to think that my family and I survived barbarous treatment and the threat of death at the hands of guerrillas just to get caught here and drown!"

Reaching the coach, Antonio Barillo stood there, obviously measuring the narrow width of the mountain road with his eyes. McCain asked him, "What about it, Antonio? Can you turn the coach around?"

Barrillo looked from the outer edge of the road, just beyond which was a sheer drop of some fifty feet, to the inside edge butted up against the towering rock wall. Finally he looked at the rising deluge below and then answered loudly, "I do not see any choice but to try, Señor McCain! It is for certain we cannot get the horses to back up that steep road!"

Lightning cracked overhead again, illuminating the gloomy mountains briefly. Then a clap of angry thunder followed.

"Okay!" McCain shouted to the driver. "We'll leave the women inside the coach, and all of us men will spread out and try to guide you as best we can!"

While Barillo was climbing to the box, Duncan Campbell stuck his head inside the window of the coach to let his wife and daughter know what was going on. Then all the men positioned themselves so they could see the edge of the road and also be seen by Antonio Barillo. Darkness would soon come. Time was of the essence.

Barillo gripped the reins with both hands, released the brake with his foot, and bent the heads of the team toward the rock wall to his right. He worked the team back and forth on the cramped, dangerous, and steep road. By repeatedly inching ahead a little, then back a little, he slowly brought the coach to where it was sitting broadside in the road. The noses of the lead horses were almost touching the rock wall in front of them.

Locking the brake for a moment, Barillo shouted down to the men, "It is going to be tricky now! I cannot see the edge of the precipice too clearly from up here, so when I back up, do not let me drop the wheels over the edge!"

"We'll watch the wheels!" McCain called back.

Barillo's teeth were clenched together in determination as he released the brake and began to coax the horses backward. John McCain and Ray Gonzales were on the vehicle's left side, while the others were on the right. As the large rear wheels rolled in reverse toward the edge, McCain peered through the wind-whipped rain, his heart beating rapidly. When the wheels were a foot from the lip of the precipice, McCain shouted, "Hold it!" at the same moment that Duncan Campbell hollered the identical order from the other side. Barillo simultaneously eased up on the reins and pulled the brake, but the rear boot of the coach hovered dangerously over the edge of the cliff.

"Okay, Antonio!" called out McCain. "Take it forward, and don't let it come back any!"

Barillo nodded, jaw tight, and placed his foot on the brake release. Reining the team to the right, he released the brake and urged the horses forward. The animals took a step, and the lead ones were nosed up against the rock wall. Over and over, Barillo backed them up a little, then sent them forward again, and little by little, the coach was becoming parallel with the narrow road.

After many such maneuvers, Antonio Barillo judged that if he backed up one more time, he could bring the vehicle all the way around the next try. He eased the team backward, and the right rear wheel moved dangerously close to the lip of the precipice. A soaking wet Duncan Campbell called out, "Careful, Antonio! You won't make it on this try! You'll have to go forward, then back up one more time!"

Nodding, Barillo reached out to grasp the long brake handle just as a lightning bolt split the air directly above the coach. The ear-splitting crack frightened the nervous animals, and they stiffened, fighting their bits, then pushed back in the harness. The stage lurched backward, and the right rear wheel slipped over the edge of the road, dropping onto the axle. At the sudden listing of the vehicle, the women inside were tumbled to the right rear corner, screaming loudly.

John McCain and Duncan Campbell rushed to the door

of the coach. Campbell calmed his wife and daughter, explaining that the coach was resting on its axle, and there was no danger of its going over the cliff.

Bending his head against the downpour, Barillo cursed under his breath and then looked back and shouted, "Is it completely down on the axle?"

"Yep!" responded McCain.

"Let me see if the horses can pull it up!" shouted Barillo. Jerking the whip from its holder, he snapped it over the horses' heads, shouting at the top of his lungs. The frightened animals strained, tugged, and snorted, but they could not budge the coach.

Ray Gonzales suddenly yelled, "Marshal! We've got to do something fast! Look!"

McCain wheeled around to find the Mexican pointing toward the raging river. It was over its banks and the boiling, roaring water was rising in their direction.

Alonzo Montoya shouted, "Marshal! The coach has to be lifted up so the team can pull it forward once the wheel is high enough to clear the lip of the edge! We've got to get under it and raise it somehow!"

The fading light of day made it difficult to see, but John McCain knelt in the mud and peered over the edge where the coach wheel was dangling. There was a narrow rock ledge directly beneath the wheel. Pointing out the ledge, he shouted above the din, "There isn't room enough for all of us to stand down there! In fact, there's only room for one man!"

Alonzo Montoya was the largest of the group, standing an inch taller than John McCain and outweighing him by fifty pounds. Stepping beside the marshal, he offered, "Let me try it! Maybe I can lift it."

Lucy Campbell had her head out the window, listening to what the men were saying. Blinking against the rain that pelted her face, she called to her father, "Mother and I will get out to lighten the load!"

Before Campbell could respond, Alonzo said, "That will

not be necessary, *señorita*. If both of you would move to the opposite corner, then your weight will make no difference."

The war secretary leaned over beside McCain and studied the small ledge. Backing away so he could look at all the men, he said, "There is no way one man can budge that coach. The way the water is rising, we'd better leave it! Let's free the horses from the stage and get out of here before we get trapped!"

"I believe I can lift it!" insisted Montoya, heading for the edge of the road. "It certainly would not hurt to give it a try!"

Lucy suddenly shoved the coach door open, telling Patricia Campbell, "I'll lighten the load, Mother. You stay in so you won't get wet."

Before Duncan Campbell could stop her, the young blonde was out in the storm, closing the door behind her. "Lucy, you be careful!" called Patricia through the window as she moved to the other corner of the coach.

Alonzo Montoya was now down on the rock ledge, ready to attempt the lift. Grabbing the end of the axle with both hands, the big husky Mexican braced his feet beneath him on the wet rock and shouted, "When I get the wheel above the edge, tell Antonio to pull the coach forward!"

"Okay!" replied McCain. "Good luck!"

Up in the box, Antonio Barillo was poised and ready. John McCain had his attention on Montoya, but when he felt something brush his sleeve, he turned to see Lucy standing beside him. He gave her a brief, reassuring smile and then looked back at Montoya.

Alonzo Montoya gritted his teeth and strained against the weight of the stagecoach. He managed to lift it nine or ten inches off the rocky shoulder of the road, but it was not sufficient to dislodge the wheel. The big Mexican let it back down, took a deep breath, and tried again. It came up about an inch higher than before, but Montoya was not able to lift it sufficiently. Setting it down, he shouted above the roar, "I cannot do it!"

As Montoya climbed back to the road, Ray Gonzales yelled, "I'll try!"

"You'd better hurry!" urged the war secretary. "That flood is moving up on us fast!"

Straining with all his might, Ray Gonzales was able to lift the coach to the same level as Alonzo had done, but it would have to come up another foot. He let it back down, and then, shaking his head in defeat, Gonzales crawled back onto the road.

Duncan Campbell shouted with urgency in his voice, "Let's unhitch the horses and get out of here! There isn't much time!"

John McCain suddenly walked toward the rear of the coach. "Might as well give it a go, too!" he said, slipping over the edge.

Patricia Campbell was watching it all from the opposite side of the coach. Yelling out a window, she asked, "Are you sure I shouldn't get out?"

McCain called back, "Just remain where you are, Mrs. Campbell!" The lawman then flexed his fingers, grasping the rounded end of the axle and making sure his feet were planted solidly beneath him. Putting every ounce of effort into his task, McCain squatted and lifted, and the wheel hovered about six inches below the surface of the road. McCain's face was beet red as he strove with all his might to lift it higher.

Taking another breath and exerting supreme effort, the marshal heaved again. After straining under the weight of the coach for nearly a minute, he finally hoisted the vehicle high enough for the wheel to clear the edge of the road. Instantly, a blend of voices bellowed at Antonio Barillo to move the coach forward. Barillo cracked the whip, shouted with authority at the team, and the stage lunged forward up the steep, muddly incline, coming to a solid rest a few feet ahead with all four wheels on the muddy ground.

Everyone cheered as the coach rolled to a stop in the middle of the road, ready to take on its passengers and climb to higher ground. U.S. Marshal John McCain hopped onto the road and was immediately pounded on the back by the exuberant men. Sidling next to him, Lucy Campbell looked at him proudly, declaring, "I knew you could do it!"

Smiling with pleasure over her praise, McCain then looked at everyone and commanded, "Hurry! Get in the coach!"

The moment everyone was back in the coach and Alonzo Montoya was seated beside him, Antonio Barillo cracked the whip and made the team heave into the harness. When they had climbed about two hundred feet, Montoya looked back in the gathering gloom. The spot where they had been stuck was now under water. Shouting down to McCain, he remarked, "Look, Marshal! We got out just in time!"

Moments later, the stage topped the incline, and Barillo found a wide spot where he could pull off the road. Although the raging flood was no longer visible, its deadly roar could still be heard.

Barillo set the brake, and then he and Alonzo Montoya scrambled down from the box to join the others inside the dry coach. John McCain heard them coming and pushed open the door, telling them, "Come on in, fellas. We'll make room for you."

Everyone shifted to accommodate the newcomers, who murmured their thanks. It was as black as pitch inside the coach, and the rain pounded the roof and the wind howled, but with the leather curtains down, no rain came in. Though they were wet and cramped, the travelers were glad to be alive and to have at least the modicum of protection afforded by the stagecoach.

Alonzo Montoya suddenly said, "I have to hand it to you, Señor McCain. I am a much larger man than you, but when it comes to strength, you are the bigger man."

"I, too, am most impressed," Ray Gonzales added.

Lucy then remarked, "Indeed, Marshal, I never knew a man could be so strong."

McCain felt his face flush.

Lucy went on. "When Father said no one could budge this coach, I was sure he was right. But when I saw how high you lifted it right off, I knew it was in you to take it the rest of the way."

A warm glow washed over the marshal. To hear such words coming from the beautiful blonde was pure satisfaction.

The rest of the group chimed in, congratulating the muscular lawman for his feat, but the praise that meant the most to U.S. Marshal John McCain was Lucy Campbell's. He was once again aware of how attracted to her he was, how beautiful he found her, how— But then the lawman reminded himself that he must stop thinking about the young woman. They lived in vastly different worlds—no doubt Lucy Campbell would one day marry some man who moved in the highest circles of Washington government—and she would never be interested in his.

Forcing his mind off thoughts of Lucy, John McCain closed his eyes and listened to the sound of the steady rainfall. Despite the cramped conditions, he soon dropped off to sleep, as did all the other weary travelers.

U.S. Marshal John McCain came awake first, and he was instantly aware of the birds singing and the absence of rain beating on the roof of the stagecoach. Pulling back a leather curtain, he saw the beginning of a sunrise against a clear sky, and he was much relieved.

McCain's legs were cramped and his back was aching and stiff from all the exertion of the day before. He needed to get out and stretch, but he would first have to awaken Antonio Barillo, for the driver was sleeping on the floor. Though he regretted having to do so, he shook Barillo, awakening him. The stirring soon had the rest of them awake as well.

Alighting from the coach with stiff limbs and muscles,

the group was happy to see that the storm was over, although they could still hear the roar of the raging stream. While the others were working off their stiffness beside the coach, John McCain walked some thirty yards away to where the road began its descent and looked at the boiling, churning water below.

Returning to the others, he announced, "The river has subsided quite a bit, but it's still over its banks. I figure it'll be this time tomorrow before we're able to get across."

Resigned, the hungry travelers soon began talking about food, but there was none on the coach. They were supposed to have been in El Sauz for supper the night before and breakfast that morning.

Ray Gonzales grinned and said, "We could go out in the woods and shoot some squirrels for breakfast."

Patricia Campbell gave him a dismal look, reminding him, "How could we cook them? There isn't a dry stick of wood to be had."

Grinning impishly, Gonzales replied, "We could just skin them and eat them real quick. At least we would have a warm meal!"

At first horrified, Patricia then apparently realized the Mexican was joking. Shaking her head, she replied good-naturedly, "I couldn't do it. At least, not without salt and pepper."

They all had a good laugh and then scattered about, sitting down on fallen logs and rocks, and letting the welcome sun warm them.

After a while, McCain said to the others, "Think I'll go take another, closer look at the river." He grinned sheepishly, adding, "I know it doesn't do any good, but at least it makes me feel somewhat useful."

"I'll go with you," Lucy declared, running her fingers through her damp hair.

Delighted at the prospect of a few minutes alone with the beautiful blonde, McCain smiled and said, "Sure. Come on." They walked down the road and soon crested the hill, out of sight of the others.

Stopping several yards past the crest, the couple looked down at the raging water. Muddy foam clung to trees and rocks where the river had risen during the night, and though it was still over its banks, the stream was definitely on the way down.

Turning to McCain, Lucy touched his arm briefly. "Marshal," she began, somewhat hesitantly, "do you mind if I ask you something personal?"

"Of course not," he replied, smiling down at her. "What is it?"

Lucy cleared her throat nervously. "Is . . . is there someone special in your life? A woman, I mean."

McCain was elated that she wanted to know. Shaking his head, he replied, "No. I've had some lady friends along the way, but there isn't anyone special." He was sure that he saw relief in her eyes, and his heart started beating faster. Letting a few seconds pass, he asked a bit apprehensively, "How about you? Is there a special man back home in Washington?"

"No," she answered quickly. "Oh, I've met nice enough men, but most of them are also dull, boring stuffed shirts. When I fall in love, it's going to be with a rugged, handsome, adventurous man."

McCain's heart was drumming against his ribs. To his ears, his voice sounded obvious as he commented, "Seems to me you'll have to hunt for your dream man somewhere outside of Washington."

"You're right about that," she responded, looking deeply into his eyes for a moment.

Then the moment passed, and McCain and Lucy headed back up the hill to rejoin the group. The lawman wanted to take the beautiful young woman at his side into his arms and tell her how relieved and pleased he was that there was no one in her life—and that she preferred someone like him. But then he told himself yet again that they were from vastly different social strata, and his elation quickly cooled.

They reached the others and were about to report on the condition of the river when a couple of the horses in the team started nickering. McCain was just turning around to look at them when suddenly six men raced up on horseback and surrounded the group, guns drawn—Felix Yorres and his cronies.

Yorres, his face swollen and scabbed, had rage in his eyes as he commanded loudly, "Nobody move!"

Then the youth whom Manual Ramos had beaten waved his gun menacingly at Ramos and spat, "You may go ahead and move, *señor*! It will give me an excuse to put a bullet in your gut!" Smirking, he added, "It is good we have so many close friends nearby. They were more than happy to lend us their weapons. Do you not agree this is a lucky thing?"

Yorres dismounted and stepped close to John McCain, snarling, "You are going to die, *gringo*! Felix Yorres will have his revenge!"

McCain stiffened and stepped away from Lucy so as to keep her from the line of fire.

After ordering one of his friends, a man named Ricardo, to collect the guns, Yorres then announced, "I am taking this dog-faced *gringo* and the beautiful *señorita* with me. The *gringo* is going to die slowly at my hands, and the *señorita* will be my woman."

Before Ricardo could follow his leader's command to get the weapons, Patricia Campbell leapt to her feet. "No!" she screamed. "You are not taking my daughter!"

Duncan Campbell jumped up beside Patricia. Eyes filled with loathing, he warned Yorres, "Don't you dare lay a hand on her!"

Yorres smiled wickedly. "And just what do you think you can do about it, *señor*?" he mocked. Glancing over his shoulder, he repeated, "Ricardo, get their guns."

McCain and his men all exchanged glances, knowing that Yorres and his bunch must not be allowed to leave with Lucy. Even though a gunfight here would be dangerous, putting the women in a position to get hit by a stray bullet, the alternative would be worse.

McCain and the others tensed up as Ricardo holstered his own weapon and approached the marshal first, to relieve him of his gun. The youthful Mexican drew up to him, a sneer on his face, but like a cat pouncing on a mouse, the marshal seized Ricardo, snatched the gun from his holster, and swung him around toward his friends. When McCain moved, the youths opened fire by reflex, and bullets ripped into Ricardo, who had suddenly become McCain's shield.

As Ricardo collapsed, McCain picked out the closest youth and fired Ricardo's gun at him, sending the slug into his windpipe at the base of his throat. He let out a gurgling cry as he went down, landing flat on his back on the muddy road.

Whipping out their own guns, McCain's men blazed away. At the same time, Duncan Campbell grabbed Patricia and Lucy by their arms, dragging them toward the stagecoach. With bullets flying, he pushed them down in the mud and rolled them under the coach, trying to put them in a place of relative safety.

Men were scattering for cover and firing at the same time. John McCain fired at Felix Yorres, hitting him in the shoulder, then had to plunge behind a tree to keep one of the other youths from shooting him. From the corner of his eye, he saw Yorres dash to his horse. With his cronies being cut down by gunfire, Yorres apparently realized his attempt to kidnap Lucy was hopeless, and he clawed his way into the saddle, losing his weapon as he did so. Panicking, Yorres spurred his mount savagely, and the startled animal bolted up the steep road, toward the raging river.

As the last of the youths fell under the defenders' guns, John McCain leapt on one of the attacker's horses and took off after Yorres. The young leader apparently heard the pursuit, for his horse was galloping toward the crest when Yorres looked back to see McCain following.

The terror that Yorres was feeling was evident. He kept a steady watch on McCain's progress until his horse crested the road and started down the steep decline. John McCain slowed his own mount before the top of the hill, and Felix Yorres was momentarily out of sight. When he went over the top, Yorres was still looking back and grinning triumphantly, evidently certain that he was maintaining enough of a lead to get away. Finally facing forward, the expression on the youth's face instantly changed to one of stark horror, and he let out a shriek at the sight of the raging river that was coming up fast.

Yorres yanked back on the reins, stiffening his legs against the stirrups, but it was too late. The galloping horse could not check its momentum, and horse and rider plunged into the rushing, churning waters. The horse went under, and Yorres was pulled from his saddle and swept away by the current.

His hysterical scream lasted only a moment before the young Mexican was smashed head-on into a huge rock that jutted up out of the boiling current. Hitting the rock with incredible force, his head split open like a ripe watermelon, splattering the rock with blood that was then immediately washed away by the turbulent waters. Felix Yorres's lifeless body flipped and spun on the surface of the raging stream, floating limply like a broken, soggy rag doll.

McCain drew up at the edge of the foamy current and watched Yorres's body until it rounded a curve and disappeared from sight. Then, reining the horse around, he started back up the road.

Chapter Nine

U.S. Marshal John McCain led the horse slowly back toward the stagecoach. His heart quickened when he saw Lucy Campbell at the crest, looking down at him with a worried expression on her face. The morning breeze toyed with her long blond hair, sweeping it over one eye, and she brushed it away. McCain stared hard at the very desirable and beautiful young woman, feeling that no female had ever stirred his emotions as she did.

When the lawman topped the incline, he swung from the saddle and stood beside Lucy. Smiling at her, he said, "I'm glad to see you're no worse for wear over this latest incident." He grinned, adding, "For a city-bred girl, you're mighty tough."

She giggled and then looked down at her muddied, torn clothes. "Too bad this dress isn't as tough as I am. I can't wait to have a bath and get into something clean." Then her face sobered and she informed him, "Yorres's friends are all dead. And Alonzo was hit in the left arm, but luckily the bullet passed clean through, missing the bone. Mother is bandaging it. She says he'll be all right."

"Good," breathed the marshal. "I'm glad none of our people were killed or hurt seriously." He wanted to add, "Especially you," but held his tongue.

As they walked together toward the others, Lucy murmured, "I saw what happened to Yorres. What an awful way to die."

McCain shrugged his broad shoulders and said tonelessly, "That it was, but it was his own fault. The world's probably better off without him."

As they neared the stagecoach, the marshal saw five corpses lying next to a tree. Alonzo Montoya was seated on a tree stump while Patricia Campbell worked on his wounded arm. Stepping beside Montoya, McCain asked, "Are you going to be all right, big fella?"

Montoya grinned. "Sí. I will be good as new when Señora Campbell gets through fixing me up."

"Maybe not quite as good as new," Patricia said with a sigh, "but you will heal up all right in time. However, this arm will have to be in a sling for a while."

McCain then suggested, "Would you rather ride inside the coach when we're able to travel again? We can put somebody else up in the box."

"I can handle it, Marshal," Montoya insisted. "I will just have to use a pistol instead of a shotgun."

Ray Gonzales suddenly interjected, "Now that you are satisfied about Alonzo, I hope you will satisfy me and tell me what happened to Felix Yorres." He gestured at the bodies, adding, "You can see that we finished off his *compadres.*"

The lawman described the youth's horrible death and then concluded, "No doubt someone will find his body somewhere down below."

"Well, at least we are rid of that bunch," Manuel Ramos said with a sigh.

Ramos's remark prompted a thought in the marshal's mind, and he turned to the war secretary, commenting, "Mr. Campbell, I've got some extra revolvers in a box under the seat of the stagecoach. Tell me, sir, have you ever used a handgun?"

Duncan Campbell nodded and replied, "Sure have, Marshal. Target shooting is one of my favorite pastimes. I have a great deal of experience with both rifles and pistols."

Looking Campbell square in the eye, McCain asked, "Would you have any problem shooting a man if it meant protecting your family or yourself? After all, a target is one thing—a human being is another."

"I assure you, Mr. McCain," Campbell said firmly, "if it meant protecting Patricia or Lucy, it would be no problem at all for me to kill a man. Nor would it be a problem if I were defending my own life. If you would like to put a gun in my hands, I will gladly take it."

Nodding, the marshal wheeled around and walked to the stagecoach. Opening the door, he leaned inside and reached under the seat, and then moments later, he returned to the war secretary, carrying a loaded Colt .45. "I didn't bring along another holster," John McCain remarked as he handed Duncan Campbell the gun, "but I would like you to keep it close for the rest of the trip. Even if we're lucky enough not to encounter Guatemalan guerrillas, we might very well come up against some more bandits like Felix Yorres and his bunch."

Gesturing with his head, the secretary asked, "How about if I take a gun belt and holster off one of Yorres's boys over there?"

"Good idea," McCain replied. "I hadn't thought about them. As a matter of fact, we might as well collect their guns and toss them under the seat with the others. We can't have too much firepower."

"I will do it, Marshal," spoke up Manuel Ramos.

"Thanks."

As soon as Ramos had removed the gun belts, the men disposed of the bodies by throwing them into the gully on the side of the road, where they tumbled down against trees and rocks far below.

The rest of the day passed quietly, and though all their stomachs were empty, they avoided the discussion of food.

Ray Gonzales and Manuel Ramos took a walk and found a bubbling spring, much to the travelers' delight. At least they had clear, fresh water to drink. The team was then led down to the rushing river and allowed to drink their fill, and when they had been led back, the saddles and bridles were removed from the young Mexicans' horses, and the animals were turned loose to roam.

John McCain and Lucy Campbell spent most of the day together, getting better acquainted. At one point, Duncan and Patricia Campbell were seated alone on a fallen tree, watching their daughter and the marshal sitting on a boulder higher up, enjoying the sunshine together. A soft breeze was whistling through the tall trees, and dozens of birds were chattering amongst the branches.

Keeping her gaze fixed on the young couple, Patricia remarked, "I think there may be something cooking up there."

Her husband smiled and nodded. "I've never seen our little girl so enchanted by a man."

"She's that, all right," agreed Patricia.

"I like him," Duncan Campbell said with conviction. "The man's got character, and he's courageous."

Patricia chuckled. "He's quite handsome, too—which surely won't hurt his cause with Lucy."

"Can't argue with that," the war secretary chortled.

Suddenly Patricia's mood changed, and she laid her head on her husband's shoulder and said, "Darling, we've got to get out of this mess safely."

"We will," Campbell responded firmly. "You just keep your chin up, honey. We will."

That night the women slept in the stagecoach while the men bedded down outside on saddle blankets taken from the Mexican bandits' horses.

At sunrise the next morning the creek was almost down to normal, and though the current was still a bit strong, Antonio Barillo pushed the nervous horses through it and

pulled up safely on the opposite side. The stage finally
rumbled into El Sauz at midmorning, and the travelers
enjoyed a hearty meal at a café while the Alegre Viaje
agent hitched a fresh six-up team to the mud-splattered
coach. John McCain allowed the women a few minutes to
freshen up inside the stage office, and soon the stage was
rolling again, heading due north. By eleven o'clock it was
on the bumpy, crooked road that wound through the
Sierra del Nido range.

As the hours passed, it was becoming evident to everyone in the coach that Lucy Campbell and John McCain
were fascinated with each other. The stage pulled into a
way station in a small, nameless mountain village at three
o'clock in the afternoon for another change of team, and all
alighted from the coach to stretch their legs. Ray Gonzales
walked over to have a private moment with McCain, who
had just returned from the privy.

Leaning against the coach, Gonzales stroked his thick
mustache, and commented, "You and the pretty *señorita*
seem to have eyes for each other. I think maybe she is
finding a place in your heart."

The marshal's face colored. Looking around to make
sure no one else was listening, he asked softly, "Am I that
obvious?"

"*Sí, señor*," chuckled the Mexican with a twinkle in his
eye, "you are as obvious as a black wart on the nose of an
albino horse. I cannot blame you, though. Señorita Campbell is quite a young lady."

McCain glanced over at the beautiful blonde, who was
exiting the station building with her mother. Taking a
deep breath and letting it out slowly, he sighed, "That she
is, Ray. That she is."

Everyone reboarded, and as the stage rolled out of the
village, rocking on its braces, Patricia Campbell asked
John McCain, "Marshal, do you think our chances of
being attacked by the Guatemalans are growing slimmer
as we move farther north?"

McCain shook his head. "I don't think so, ma'am. I wish it were true that with every passing mile we get farther from the possibility of such danger, but I don't think we can let our guard down for a moment."

Ray Gonzales spoke up. "The Guatemalans have a very mysterious network across our country, Señora Campbell. No one knows how their system works, but we have seen them keep up with each other concerning things that are going on hundreds of miles apart. They are very smart people. The marshal is right. We dare not relax for one minute."

Her face grim, Patricia touched her husband's arm and nodded.

"The thing is," said McCain, "there's no way of knowing how long it took the guerrillas in the Chihuahua area to learn of the assault on the mansion. Before we launched the attack, I told Ray and his men to be sure they killed every guerrilla on the place, preventing any of them from getting away to carry the news to other Guatemalans nearby. This definitely bought us time, but how much time, there's no way of knowing. Sooner or later, other guerrillas are bound to drop by the mansion to see their pals—maybe even to check on how it went with getting their countrymen in New Orleans set free."

Patricia's face was rigid. "So there's a good possibility they'll be riding up on us at any time."

"There is that possibility, ma'am," McCain admitted. "But then again, even if they have learned of the assault by now, they still have to find us."

"And the marshal's idea of using a stagecoach will make that much more difficult to do, darling," Duncan Campbell told his wife encouragingly.

McCain grinned and said, "The idea wasn't mine, sir. It was actually Chief U.S. Marshal Eldridge Harris in El Paso who came up with it. I just agreed with him and have been the one to make it work. At least it's worked so far. I'm convinced that if the Guatemalans are searching for us, they're combing the back country looking for a group traveling on horseback. But as I said, we have to remain alert."

The stage dropped down into a deep canyon and then climbed out and hit a long, level stretch that lay between two mountain ranges. It was breathtaking country with lush green meadows dotted with wildflowers of every color. Heavy timber fringed the valley on both sides, swooping up from the foothills all the way to the shoulders of the great snowcapped peaks on the east and the west.

Staring out her window, Lucy Campbell's mind was not so much on the scenery as it was on John McCain. She savored the times they had been spending together—times that she believed almost made this entire ordeal worthwhile. The lawman's effect on her was powerful enough to be felt even when they were not looking at each other or speaking. Though the young woman was keenly aware of the imminent danger that hovered over the stagecoach like a dark cloud, somehow she had an inward peace—and she knew its source. John McCain's presence and his tenderness toward her cushioned her fears.

The lovely blonde watched the scenery roll by and asked herself, *Could this feeling I have for John be love? I've often thought it must feel something akin to this, but how can I know for sure? And even if I believe it is, will I have time enough with him to be really positive? If all goes well, this trip will be over in a few days, and Mother and Father and I will go back to Washington, John will take on another assignment, and perhaps soon he'll be in a situation similar to this with some other woman—and show the same tenderness toward her as he is showing me.*

As repugnant as the thought was, Lucy told herself that she had no right to think John McCain might be feeling as strongly toward her as she was feeling toward him. He was such a gentleman, he probably treated every young woman exactly the same way.

Lucy's thoughts were interrupted by the sudden slowing of the stage. Antonio Barillo shouted down from the box, "Marshal!"

"What is it?" McCain called back.

"There is a group of perhaps a dozen men on horseback sitting near the edge of the timber off to the right. What should I do?"

Tensing, McCain leaned over and peered out the window on the right side of the coach and spotted the riders about a quarter mile away. Returning to his seat, he hollered up to the driver, "Just keep going at a steady pace! We'll be ready in here. If they start toward us, let me know. I'll tell you what to do at that point!"

Reaching under the seat, McCain began pulling out rifles, giving one to each man, including Duncan Campbell. Looking at mother and daughter, he said, "Ladies, if those riders attack, I want you both to get down on the floor and stay as low as you can. These doors have been plated with iron, and you'll be protected down there."

Patricia Campbell clung to her husband. Duncan Campbell squeezed her arm reassuringly and then looked at his daughter, who was proving to be the stronger of the two, and softly suggested, "Honey, you help your mother cope if shooting starts."

Lucy nodded, tight lipped.

They all sat bolt upright, their bodies rigid with tension and fear. With each passing moment, the air inside the coach seemed to thicken as the travelers' worry increased. Then Antonio Barillo laughed, shouting down, "It's all right! The riders are driving a herd of cattle—which at this very moment are wading in a small stream, taking their fill of water." He laughed again, adding, "The horsemen are only Mexican cowboys!"

Tears filmed Patricia's eyes. With quivering lips, she gasped, "Thank God!"

The occupants of the coach pressed toward the windows

on the right side of the coach to get a glimpse of the riders as they drew abreast of them. The cowboys took off their hats and waved, and the passengers waved back, smiling and calling greetings to them.

"Whew!" breathed Duncan Campbell, settling back in his seat. "It sure would help if Guatemalans looked different from Mexicans, wouldn't it?"

Ray Gonzales laughed, relief evident on his face. "Actually, you can tell us apart up close, Señor Campbell."

The secretary's brow furrowed. "Really?"

"Sí," Gonzales answered. "The Guatemalans have a mean look in their eyes. We Mexicans do not."

Tugging on his mustache, John McCain chuckled and then declared, "Oh yeah? If Davy Crockett, Jim Bowie, and the other boys who were at the Alamo were still around, I'd like to hear what they'd say about that!"

Ray Gonzales grinned crookedly, and everybody had a good laugh.

Continuing on without further incident, the Alegre Viaje stagecoach rocked and swayed its way northward. Later in the day they found themselves passing the towering peak of Cerro del Barrison, the red glow of the sun making the jagged peak look as though it was ready to catch fire.

Antonio Barillo reined the horses to a halt and set the brake and then climbed down from the box. Sticking his head through the window beside John McCain, he said, "The map given to me by Julio Herrera shows that the next way station is in the town of El Sueco, where there are supposed to be a couple of very nice hotels. Unfortunately, we are still a number of miles from El Sueco. Shall we pull over for the night and make camp, or should we push on to El Sueco?"

"Just a minute, Antonio," McCain said. Turning toward the others in the coach, he asked them, "Would you folks rather rough it somewhere along the road for the night, or sleep in a nice clean hotel bed and have something to eat besides?"

The quick response to continue on was exactly what McCain figured it would be. "Okay," he responded. "We ought to be in El Sueco by eight o'clock, if Antonio is as good a driver as he thinks he is."

Manuel Ramos laughed and said jokingly, "Then we will probably not be there until midnight, Señor McCain!"

Even the harried Patricia Campbell laughed, and the smiles on their faces said that they all felt good to do so.

It was shortly before eight o'clock when the stagecoach rolled into El Sueco. The Alegre Viaje agent, who had been worried about the coach's delay and was happy to see it finally arrive, directed them to the best hotel, and the travelers made their way there and checked in. Patricia and Lucy were in a room together on the second floor, with Duncan Campbell and Manuel Ramos on one side of them, while Alonzo Montoya shared a room with Ray Gonzales on the other side. John McCain and Antonio Barillo took a room directly across the hall from the room where the women were staying.

Having established their sleeping quarters, the women were especially happy to have the opportunity to bathe. Thanks to the thoughtfulness of the general store's proprietor, who had opened up his business even at this late hour, they were able to put on new clothing. Then the travelers eagerly went to the hotel's restaurant and found to their delight that the food was delicious. When the meal was finished, everyone stood up and headed back into the hotel's lobby, where Antonio Barillo suggested, "I would like to go to that cantina we passed a few doors down for a little while."

"Me, too," said Manuel Ramos. "It would be good to hear some music and have a drink. How about you, Alonzo? You want to come?"

"No, thank you," replied Montoya, shaking his head. "My arm is hurting. I need to rest."

Ray Gonzales took a step closer to Ramos and Barillo and said, "Maybe you two should not go, either. You need clear heads at all times to stay alert—and a hangover would not give you that."

Ramos said, "We will only have one little drink, Ray. We promise, don't we, Antonio?"

"Sí," Antonio agreed. "Just one little drink. Mainly we would just like to get in on the fun. Okay?"

Gonzales turned to McCain and asked, "What do you think, John?"

McCain rubbed his chin and replied, "Sometimes trouble starts in cantinas—and the last thing we need is trouble. There's potentially enough of that without inviting more. Frankly, I don't know you fellas well enough to be confident you'll stop with only one drink."

"Ray knows us well enough, Marshal," Ramos countered. "When we say we will have only one drink, we mean it."

Duncan Campbell spoke up. "Marshal, if my opinion counts for anything, I say let them go. They've had a hard journey so far, and they're entitled to a little relaxation." Shrugging, he added, "In fact, it might even do them good—provided they don't have too much to drink."

Manuel Ramos smiled broadly and elbowed Barillo. "See there, Antonio! The secretary of war is a very intelligent man!"

John McCain snickered, shaking his head. "Okay, okay, you guys," he said. "If Ray approves, I'll go along with it."

"What about it, Ray?" asked Barillo.

"I will tell you what. I will go along and make sure that you both keep your promise—and I can also make sure you stay no longer than an hour."

The Campbells, Montoya, and McCain went up to the second floor and bid each other good night before heading into their respective rooms. McCain started turning the knob to his door when Lucy softly called to him, "Good night, Marshal McCain."

McCain smiled and said, "Miss Campbell, if you wouldn't think me too forward, I'd like you to call me John."

"On one condition," she replied.

"And that is?"

"I'd like you to call me Lucy."

Nodding emphatically, he agreed, "It will be my pleasure. Good night, Lucy."

She smiled sweetly and then responded, "Good night, John."

McCain waited until she had closed the door and he heard the lock turn before he entered his room. His heart was beating against his ribs again, and there was almost a physical ache in his arms, he wanted to hold her so desperately. Taking a deep breath and letting it out slowly, he tossed his hat on the dresser and then removed his gun belt and hung it on a bedpost at the head of the bed. He had left a lamp burning low on a bedstand, and he turned it up slightly.

Walking to the open window, he stuck his head out and enjoyed the cool night air. From the window, McCain could hear the sounds from the cantina echoing off the adobe walls of the buildings lining the street.

Pulling his head inside, the marshal sat down on the edge of the bed. He knew he could not retire for the night until the three Mexicans were in their respective rooms, and even if he did drift off to sleep, Antonio Barillo would most certainly disturb him when he came in. McCain decided he would just stretch out on the bed and rest his weary bones until the men returned and they could all get some much-needed sleep.

The federal lawman lifted a foot to remove his right boot when there was a light tap on his door. Grabbing the Colt .45 from its holster, he thumbed back the hammer and walked across the room. Turning the knob and cracking the door enough to see who was knocking, he was surprised to see Lucy Campbell smiling at him.

"H-hello," he said, widening the door's gap and suddenly finding it difficult to breathe.

In a half whisper, the captivating blonde said, "I'm not really sleepy yet. Are you?"

"No. I was just going to stretch out on the bed and wait till the men return."

"Well," Lucy said, clearly trying not to display her nervousness, "I thought if you weren't sleepy either, maybe we could talk for a few minutes. It . . . it will have to be brief. Mother said it would not be improper for me to visit you if I stayed only a few minutes. Five to be exact."

"Come in," he quickly offered and then closed the door quietly behind her as she entered. "Sit down," McCain suggested, pointing to an overstuffed chair near the window. Easing the hammer down on the gun, he slipped the Colt back in its holster.

Lucy sat in the chair and folded her hands in her lap, while the marshal sat on the edge of the bed.

There was a moment of silence. A bit off balance, McCain hurried to fill the void, asking, "Was there anything special you wanted to talk about?"

Lucy cleared her throat lightly. "Yes."

"All right," he said gently, "what is it?"

Her brow furrowed. "I . . . I hope you won't think me too forward, but I just wanted to tell you that I have mixed emotions about this trip being over."

"What do you mean?"

"I mean"—she paused and sighed—"I mean I'll be glad when the strain of the danger is past and my parents and I are safe in our own country. But . . . but . . ."

John McCain's heart was in his throat. "But what?"

She looked down at her hands. "I . . . dread for the day to come when I won't be seeing you any more."

Touched deeply, McCain stood up and looked down with tender eyes at the beautiful young woman. Lucy stood as well, looking up and holding his gaze as he said, "I may just as well come clean, little lady. The same kind of dread is eating away at me."

"Really?"

"Yes, ma'am. And as long as you're here and I have this opportunity, I might as well tell you the whole truth. I . . . I think I'm falling in love with you, Lucy."

Lucy Campbell's eyes widened. Taking a half step toward him, she admitted, "That's what I feel, too, John. I've never been in love before, and . . . and there's a lot about it I don't know. But I think I'm falling in love with you."

Suddenly they were both out of words. McCain opened his aching arms and folded her to him. He locked her tight against his chest for a long moment and then held her at arm's length. Their eyes met, and her face was expectant and radiant in the pale lamplight that filled the room with a soft yellow glow. Lucy closed her eyes, and their lips came together in a magic, velvety kiss. Forgotten was the imminent danger of prowling Guatemalan guerrillas. Forgotten were the long hard miles that lay ahead before the Campbell family would be safe. For a blissful moment, Lucy Campbell and John McCain were in a place without care or worry.

When they parted and they returned to the real world, he smiled and said, "I'm sorry for all the trouble and anguish you and your parents have had to go through . . . but I have to say I'm glad it happened. If it hadn't, I would never have met you."

"Life is like that," she said in return. "Sometimes the greatest blessings come from the biggest heartaches. I'm glad it happened, too."

John McCain kissed the beautiful blonde again and then, though it grieved him to point it out, said, "I think your five minutes are up."

Lucy nodded silently and headed for the door. Opening it, McCain checked the hall to make sure it was safe and then looked at her lovingly and said softly, "Good night, little lady."

"Good night," she said softly.

He watched Lucy step to her room and tap on the door. Patricia opened it, and the young woman slipped inside. Turning, Lucy smiled at the tall, handsome lawman and then closed the door behind her.

Sighing happily, John McCain strode across to the window, parted the curtains, and looked up at the twinkling stars. As he stood there, letting the night breeze play with his hair, he thought that he had never known anything as sweet as the taste of Lucy's kisses on his lips.

Chapter Ten

U.S. Marshal John McCain lay on the bed, listening to the music and laughter from the cantina floating on the night air. When a full hour had passed and Ray Gonzales and his men had yet to return, McCain rose from the bed and began to pace the floor. When another quarter hour had gone by, the marshal feared that something had gone wrong, and he decided there was nothing to do now but go to the cantina himself and see what was going on.

He put on his boots and was buckling his gun belt when he realized that the music had stopped. He could clearly hear loud voices mixed with laughter, and it sounded like the occupants were cheering. Stepping out into the hallway, he walked across and tapped on Duncan Campbell's door. There were muffled footsteps, and then the door came open, and the war secretary stood there in his socks.

Looking into McCain's eyes, Campbell asked, "You're worried, too, eh?"

"Yes. I'm going—"

A door came open farther down the hall, and Alonzo Montoya stepped out of his room and walked quickly toward the lawman. Montoya declared, "Ray and the others should be back by now."

Nodding, McCain said, "I was just telling Mr. Campbell that I'm going over to the cantina and see what's happened to them."

"I will get my gun and go with you," the big Mexican declared, turning away.

"That won't be necessary, Alonzo," the marshal countered.

Montoya stopped, pivoted, and argued, "I don't think you should go alone, Marshal."

"I have to. You and Mr. Campbell will have to make sure the women are safe. One man alone here is not enough protection."

Duncan Campbell ran a quivering hand through his salt-and-pepper hair. Then, shaking his head, he said, "John, I'm sorry I encouraged you to let them go over there. Maybe we've had Guatemalans following the stagecoach without our realizing it, and they've captured Ray and his men. If that's the case, they'll be heading for this hotel next."

Abruptly there was the sound of boots pounding rapidly up the stairs. Drawing his revolver, McCain waited tensely. Then Antonio Barillo appeared, charging down the hall toward them. "Marshal!" gasped the Mexican as he ran. "We have real trouble!"

Coming to a halt, Barillo continued breathlessly, "Manuel got into an argument with a mountain-sized man at the cantina, and when Ray stepped in to settle the argument, the huge man knocked him down! Four of the man's friends are now holding Ray on the floor while the big man is beating up Manuel!"

Patricia and Lucy came out of their room, worry showing on their faces. "What's going on?" asked Patricia, her voice uncertain.

"Trouble at the cantina, honey," answered her husband. "You and Lucy go back inside and lock your door."

"Guatemalans?" gasped Patricia, trembling fingers going to her gaping mouth.

"No, just Mexicans. But Manuel is apparently about to be pounded to a pulp by a giant of a man."

John McCain's eyes blazed with anger. "I was afraid of just this kind of thing happening." He sighed and then ordered, "You ladies get back in your room. Mr. Campbell, I'll leave Antonio and Alonzo with you. Keep your guns in hand and watch this hallway carefully until I get back."

"Oh, John!" exclaimed Lucy. "You shouldn't go alone!"

Pausing, McCain eyed Lucy tenderly and replied, "Don't worry. I'll be all right. It won't be the first time I've encountered uneven odds"—he gave her a crooked grin— "and so far I've always come out on top." With that, he turned and bolted down the hall and then took the stairs three at a time.

Running out of the hotel, McCain hurried along the broad, dusty street to the cantina. Storming through the squeaky batwing doors, John McCain was ready for trouble—and he found it. The scene was exactly as Antonio Barillo had described it. Ray Gonzales had been disarmed and was being held on the floor by four stout men. Gonzales's nose was bleeding, and when he glanced up and saw John McCain, there was both fear and anger on his rugged face.

The lawman shifted his gaze to the end of the long, rough-hewn bar, where a massive bearded Mexican had Manuel Ramos at his mercy. Ramos was seated on the bar with his legs dangling over the front edge, while two muscular Mexicans, whom McCain figured were the cantina's bartenders, held his arms behind his back from where they stood behind the bar. Though Ramos's skin was dark, the marshal could see that his cheeks were inflamed from being struck repeatedly, and blood oozed from his nostrils and from a corner of his mouth.

The huge man suddenly swore at Ramos, slapped him several times and then stepped back and roared with laughter. The crowd, which was clearly backing the huge Mexican, laughed with him and applauded, punctuating their praise with whistles and cheers.

Ramos finally caught sight of McCain, and his eyes pleaded for help. Though he was a tough individual, his opponent seemed almost twice his size, leaving Ramos at a clear disadvantage.

The place was filled with patrons, including many women, most of whom were heavily painted and wore flowers in their hair. The mariachi band was seated on a small platform at one end of the bar, but the present excitement was taking precedence over their talents, and they sat in silence, holding their instruments on their laps. Although McCain had burst noisily through the batwings, he remained virtually unnoticed by all except his two friends.

Turning to one of the bystanders, McCain asked, "What is the big man's name?"

"Jorge Cortez," came the quick reply.

Cortez began battering Ramos's face again. McCain immediately sized up the man and the situation. Cortez was wearing a sidearm, but the marshal decided against drawing his gun on him. Such a move would be suicide, for nearly every man in the smoke-filled place was armed—and no doubt would side with Jorge Cortez.

McCain knew, however, that all men liked to see a good fight, and probably no one would interfere if he took on the giant with his fists. To do so would challenge Jorge's pride. If McCain won, undoubtedly there would be enough respect garnered from the crowd to allow him and his friends to walk out unmolested.

But it was a big if. The monster stood a good three inches taller than the lawman and outweighed him by at least a hundred pounds.

The crowd was applauding Cortez again as he backed away from Manuel Ramos and accepted a bottle of whiskey from a bystander. Ramos's face was swelling and there was more blood coming from his nose and mouth. The sight of it replenished McCain's anger, and with his blood hot, he detached himself from the crowd and stepped toward the huge Mexican, who had his back to him with the whiskey bottle tipped up to his mouth.

Stopping about ten feet away, the lawman bellowed,

"Cortez!" His voice cut through the large room, and every eye in the place suddenly focused on the *gringo* who stood with his legs spread and his fists balled.

Jorge Cortez lowered the bottle and slowly wheeled around, smacking his lips, and a hush came over the place. Cortez looked McCain up and down, regarding him as if he were something repugnant. "You wanted something from me, cockroach?" he asked with a curled lip. "What would a cockroach *gringo* want with Jorge?" His voice was so deep, it sounded as though it were coming from the bowels of a cave.

John McCain felt a chill run down his spine as he took in the expanse of the bearded monster's chest and shoulders. The man was indeed a mountain—but McCain had already cast the die. Letting his anger dispel the fear, he gritted his teeth and rasped, "Yeah, I want something, all right. I want all these people in here to see you for what you really are: A coward! Any man who would beat up someone half his size is a pathetic coward! And you are doubly a coward for having your friends hold your opponent's hands so he cannot fight back fairly!"

Jorge Cortez's face went black with rage. Slamming the bottle on the bar, he turned and faced McCain squarely. Fixing the marshal with a pair of watery but murderous eyes, he sneered wickedly. "Men much larger than you have dared irritate me. They now lie in their graves. I will not even have to work up a sweat to kill you."

Ready for what was coming, McCain snarled, "*After* you do it, you can brag about it, yellow-belly!"

An eerie stillness settled over the cantina as the onlookers waited to watch their champion take on his challenger. John McCain tensed, also waiting. Cortez spit on the floor and then bared his teeth and charged at McCain like a maddened bull. But the lithe lawman sidestepped him, and Cortez's momentum carried him across the floor in an awkward stumble, and he smashed into two of the men who were holding Ray Gonzales on the floor, knocking them rolling. The other two let go of Gonzales and scattered for safer territory while Cortez kept going, slamming into the wall. Immediately getting up, Gonzales joined the crowd and began cheering the marshal on.

Jorge Cortez got to his feet and charged again. Timing his move, McCain dropped to the floor and rolled toward the giant, and Cortez's huge feet tangled in the marshal's body. He went down hard, shaking the building. As he regained his stance, the hatred he felt toward his opponent for getting the better of him was evident on his face. Roaring with fury, he attacked.

John McCain planted his feet, ready to punch, for he could not keep up the evasive tactics all night. The battle had to come to blows. Jorge Cortez reached him and swung a haymaker, but McCain ducked it and surprised the monster by banging him hard on the jaw. Cortez's head snapped back, and when it bounded forward, McCain popped him with a stiff left jab, then followed quickly with a second smashing right to the jaw.

The huge man staggered slightly and then closed in, punching. One of his massive fists only glanced off McCain's head, but the marshal still felt its effect, and tiny points of light lit up inside his head. Recovering, McCain managed to pound Cortez's nose, but then he caught a blow on his own temple, and he felt his feet leave the floor. He came down on top of a table that had wisely been vacated by its occupants a moment earlier. The legs of the table gave way, and it crashed to the floor, sending chairs bouncing in three directions.

Instead of tiny points of light, McCain now had what seemed to be meteors shooting through his brain. He rolled off the top of the table, shaking his head in an attempt to clear it, and vaguely heard the crowd egging their champion on. Turning his head, he saw Cortez coming after his prey, fists cocked, and the lawman knew he had to avoid those deadly hands. He leapt to his feet and ducked a whistling blow, then savagely popped Cortez's thick lips. The upper lip split and spurted blood. As McCain jumped back to escape another haymaker the giant paused long enough in his pursuit to wipe his right forearm across his mouth. When he saw the blood from his lip, a wildness filled his eyes. "I'm going to kill you, little man!" he bawled.

McCain darted in, surprising the Mexican, and tattooed him with six rapid blows to the mouth and nose. When he danced back, dodging both punches that Cortez swung at him, he saw that the man's bottom lip was now also split, and his beard was coated with blood.

The marshal was finding his range, and he was fully aware that his Sunday punch was not going to knock the monster out. Jorge Cortez would have to be chopped down a little at a time—as a woodsman drops a stalwart, towering tree with his ax.

A woman in the crowd shouted, "Pound the *gringo* into the floor, Jorge!" The command elicited a rousing cheer from most of the other patrons.

Spurred by the encouragement from his backers, the massive Mexican rumbled after the smaller lawman, determination in his eyes. As the two men continued to grapple, battling for supremacy, it was clear that the onlookers were surprised that John McCain could hold himself as well as he did.

Ducking a right cross and countering with two quick left jabs to Cortez's mouth, the marshal once again caught the giant up short. But then Jorge caught him on the shoulder as he was backing away, and pain shot all the way down McCain's arm and across his shoulders. His back was to the bar, where the two men still held Manuel Ramos in their grasp, and Jorge came on the run, intending to ram his smaller opponent into the bar.

McCain leapt out of the way at the last second, and the giant smashed into the bar. Ramos managed to raise his legs and twist sideways to avoid getting hit as Cortez's stomach hit the hard wood with such force that his breath gushed out of him. Pulling himself together, he swore, pivoting around—only to find John McCain waiting for him and pelting him with two massive blows.

The giant recovered and swung wildly, connecting with McCain's jaw. Before the lawman could fully recover, Cortez picked up a chair and lifted it high over his head, about to smash it down on McCain's head. But the marshal managed to get out of the way, and instead of the lawman's head, the chair took out another table.

Leaping onto his much larger opponent, McCain fought back gamely, sometimes gaining ground momentarily, then sometimes losing it. At one point he was slammed onto the hard wooden floor, and the wind was knocked out of him while above him, the candles in the wagon-wheel chandeliers whirled in a fuzzy circle. The crowd roared its approval, then suddenly a monstrous form loomed over McCain like some gigantic bird, about to jump on top of him. But he adeptly rolled in time to escape the nearly three hundred pounds of revenge-seeking man, and Cortez landed on the floor with a crash.

Grabbing a leg from one of the smashed tables, Jorge Cortez wielded it like a club, clearly determined to finished the agile *gringo* off. He swung it over his head, but again McCain leapt out of harm's way, while the momentum carried the giant into the wall. Cortez swore, regained his balance, and moved in again. The marshal sidestepped him, and the table leg thundered down on the top of the bar with a deafening crack. The leg splintered and left a permanent dent in the bar.

The monster whirled around, still gripping the splintered table leg. Menacing McCain with the sharp, pointed end, Cortez snarled, "I'm going to run this through your heart, *gringo* cockroach!"

Countering with a weapon of his own, McCain held a chair out in front of him, legs forward. The huge Mexican merely laughed sardonically as he charged, but the lawman hit him with the chair, shattering it, and the blow knocked the table leg from Cortez's hands. It hit the floor and slid under a row of tables, disappearing from sight.

Snarling dangerously, the giant lashed out at the lawman, but McCain ducked the punch, and Cortez's fist hit the wall with such force that it cracked the adobe—as well as the bones in his hand. He swore furiously and spun around, then threw his weight against McCain, and suddenly the lawman felt himself turned around and seemingly gripped in a vise. His feet were off the floor as the gargantuan man had John McCain in a deadly bear hug. Even though Cortez had to favor the broken hand, his grasp was still unbelievably strong, and McCain felt the breath leave his lungs, while his ribs were close to popping. Knowing he was in deep trouble if he did not break the powerful hold, the lawman gritted his teeth and threw back both hands, planting a thumb in each of the monster's eyes. Cortez wailed and tried to shake the thumbs loose from his eyes, but McCain had a firm grip.

Screaming wildly, Cortez threw McCain through the air. The marshal sailed into several bystanders, knocking them down. Getting to his feet, McCain found the giant was holding his good hand to his eyes, staggering around like a blind man.

The marshal knew the time had come to finish the Mexican off, and he went after him like a hungry wolf. He planted his feet and cracked the huge man with two vicious, telling blows that took Jorge Cortez by surprise. The crowd gasped as he went down.

The marshal stood over him, breathing hard, waiting for him to get up. His legs wobbling, Cortez groped his way to his feet while rubbing at his bloodshot eyes and blinking. Catching a brief glimpse of his opponent, fury coursed through Cortez's veins. Clearly determined to kill his antagonist, he went after McCain, although the broken fist kept him from further punching.

This time U.S. Marshal John McCain sent a sledgehammer blow at the huge man's head that stopped him cold.

Jorge Cortez went down flat on his back and stayed there, unconscious.

Sucking for air, McCain turned and faced the bar. McCain ran his hot gaze over the faces of the two men holding Manuel Ramos and growled, "You saw your hero whipped fair and square. I would say I have won my friend's release." Giving each other a quick glance, the men relinquished their hold on Ramos, and he hopped down off the bar and headed toward the door where Ray Gonzales stood smiling and shaking his head in amazement.

Striding toward the batwings, McCain was forced to stop by a ring of hostile patrons blocking his way. Pulling himself up to his full height, he announced coldly, "My friends and I are leaving. I suggest you do not try to stop us." Dark eyes studied the rugged American for a brief moment, and then the line broke, clearing a path to the doorway. John McCain and his companions moved out onto the street and headed for the hotel.

When the Alegre Viaje stagecoach rolled out of El Sueco the next morning, Lucy Campbell looked with love and concern at John McCain's bruised and battered face. At breakfast, Manuel Ramos and Ray Gonzales had given everyone a blow-by-blow description of the fight, and the lovely blonde was especially proud of the lawman's prowess. She had never known a man like him.

It was coming up on noon when the stage pulled into the town of Moctezuma. While the horses were being changed, Antonio Barillo consulted his map, and when the travelers were about to board the stage for the next leg of the trip, Barillo smiled at them and exclaimed, "I have good news! We are now exactly halfway to Juárez!"

McCain and Lucy looked intently at each other, and each knew what the other was thinking. When the second half of the journey was over, they would have to part.

The coach rolled on, and by nightfall it was parked behind the Alegre Viaje office in the little town of Rosita.

The weary travelers took rooms in Rosita's hotel and then had supper together at the town's only café.

After the meal, John McCain and Lucy Campbell took a stroll in the moonlight to the northern edge of town. Crickets filled the night with their music, and the sweet scent of flowers was in the air. Stopping alongside a rail fence, the lawman took hold of the blonde's hands and looked down into her eyes. He did not say anything, but Lucy had apparently read the message on his face.

"John, you're having the same trouble I am, aren't you?" she asked quietly.

"You mean that we're soon going to have to part?"

"Yes."

"Of course," he admitted. "But there's something else."

Squeezing the strong hands that held hers, she asked, "What is it?"

"I no longer think I'm falling in love with you, Lucy. I know it."

Her ripe mouth curved in a smile. "And you're concerned about how I feel? Well, as long as we're bringing things up to date . . . I don't think it anymore, either, darling. I know I am falling in love with *you!*"

Folding her into his arms, John McCain kissed her tenderly and then said, "Lucy, there's one thing I need to discuss with you."

Looking deep into his eyes, she asked, "Yes?"

"It's"—he hesitated momentarily—"well, it's the fact that we come from two different worlds. You're on a much higher social level than I, as a mere federal marshal, am. When I think of what the future might hold for us, well, I'm not sure if—"

"John," Lucy cut in, "we may come from two different worlds, as you put it, but that has nothing to do with what the future might hold for us. High society is for me nothing but an empty shell. I'm proud of what Father is, of course, but to be honest, I am bored to death living among the so-called elite crowd. I told you I would have to find the man of my dreams somewhere outside of Washington—and I have. I want my future to be with you. And as for your being a 'mere federal marshal,' well, where would our country be without brave men like you to keep us safe? I love you for what you are, and I would not change one thing about you . . . including your social status."

"But what about your parents? Certainly their plans for your future include your marrying a man they consider to be on their social level."

"My parents are wonderful people, John," she breathed, "and they do not plan my future. I have a life of my own, and they will not try to live it for me. All they want for me is that I be happy."

With his heart pounding for love of Lucy Campbell, John McCain took her in his arms and kissed her again. When he released her, he told her breathlessly, "We better get back to the hotel. Tomorrow's another long, hard day."

The next morning the stage left Rosita at six o'clock. The next stop was to be at the way station in Villa Ahumada, some fifteen miles farther north. Spirits were rising among the travelers, for they were now just ninety miles from Juárez. The coach was out of the mountains and moving across level ground, where the horses could make better time.

John McCain sat across from the stunning blonde, devouring her beauty with his eyes. When his gaze strayed to Patricia, who sat next to her daughter, McCain saw that the strain of the trip was taking its toll on her. Desiring to ease it by giving her some encouragement, he said, "Mrs. Campbell, this ordeal will soon be over for you, and I'm sure our luck will keep holding and we'll escape any further run-ins with guerrillas. After all, we've encountered no Guatemalans, and we're just two days from Juárez."

Patricia's furrowed brow relaxed, and she gave the lawman a weak smile. She looked at her husband and then at John, and said, "Your optimism is comforting to me, John. Thank you."

The stage rolled into Villa Ahumada at nine o'clock, and it was not quite nine-thirty when it was on the road once more behind a fresh six-up team. They had gone some three or four miles when Alonzo Montoya suddenly stiffened in the seat. Antonio Barillo followed his shotgunner's eyes, and his heart froze. Immediately he slowed the stagecoach.

Directly in front of them, blocking their passage, was a large band of swarthy, armed men. They were off their horses, standing in a straight line across the road, and each man held a rifle and wore at least one revolver on his hip. Huge boulders lined the road on both sides, making it impossible to go around the men. The only other alternative was to turn the stage around and ride hard back for Villa Ahumada.

Barillo called down, "Marshal!"

Tilting up his head alongside the window, McCain shouted, "Yes?"

"We've got trouble. Take a look up ahead."

Quickly McCain stuck his head out the window, as did the other men.

When the marshal saw the men lined across the road, rifles ready, his body went rigid. "Guatemalans!" he gasped.

Patricia Campbell began to whimper, putting a trembling hand over her mouth.

McCain judged the guerrillas to be about four hundred yards ahead. While he pondered the situation, Barillo called from up top, "Shall I turn us around and head for Villa Ahumada, Marshal?"

A few seconds passed, and then McCain replied, "No, Antonio. That would only invite disaster. There's no way the stage can outrun men on horseback. Look, you make it appear as if you're going to stop the coach, and we'll be ready with our weapons in here. When you're about twenty yards from the guerrillas, crack the whip over the horses' heads and plow through the line. The team is fresh, so they can give it a good run. If we can injure some of them, we'll have a better chance when the rest come in pursuit."

"Okay," Barillo agreed. "Get yourselves ready."

Duncan Campbell immediately put his wife and daughter on the floor, where Patricia Campbell went into hysterics.

"It'll never be over until we're dead, Duncan!" she screamed. "Those beasts will never rest until they've killed us—and that's what they intend to do! They're going to kill us!"

Chapter Eleven

While Duncan Campbell tried to calm his wife, the other men levered cartridges into the chambers of their repeater rifles. When they were all fully loaded, U.S. Marshal John McCain broke out the small box of dynamite, muttering that his words of optimism had apparently come too soon.

Her face pinched with fear, Patricia Campbell finally took a ragged breath, telling her husband, "I'm sorry for behaving so badly, Duncan. I don't know what came over me. I'm just so frightened—and I thought we were safe."

"I know, honey. But I daresay John is no novice at fighting for his life, nor are the rest of these men. And now I've got to focus my attention on helping them as much as I can." He looked deep into her eyes, asking, "Do you understand?"

Closing her eyes, Patricia Campbell nodded and then let out a shaky, "Yes."

Lucy grasped her mother's upper arms and said calmly, "Just stay down, Mother. We'll be all right."

McCain was stuffing sticks of dynamite into a shirt pocket when he paused and reached for Lucy's hand. Squeezing it, he told her comfortingly, "We'll get out of this, my love. I promise."

Suddenly his face reddened, and he looked up to see Duncan Campbell eyeing him closely. Shrugging, he admitted, "I am in love with your daughter, sir. There's no sense hiding it—especially not now."

Tears filled Lucy's blue eyes, and she looked first at her mother and then at her father. "You don't mind, do you?" she asked Duncan Campbell. "You see, I love him, too."

Campbell grinned. "It doesn't surprise me in the least, my dear. Your mother and I saw it coming days ago."

Lucy was clearly taken aback. "Oh!" she exclaimed. She was about to say more when the coach began to slow as it approached the armed men. Immediately she and Patricia clung to each other, and all other thoughts were crowded out by their dire situation.

Bracing himself, the war secretary hefted his rifle and gave the lawman a quick look. "We're in your hands now, John," he said.

"And the Almighty's," McCain added.

The coach gave a sudden lurch forward, gaining immediate speed as Barillo cracked his whip over the horses' heads and bellowed, "Heeyah!"

Peering out the window, John McCain could see that the abrupt, unexpected action took the phalanx of men off guard as the big, powerful horses bolted toward them. The coach slammed into five of the men as the others leapt from danger. Three of those who felt the violent collision with thundering horseflesh were sent flying by the impact. The others screamed as they were trampled by the pounding hooves.

Up in the box, Alonzo Montoya unleashed his revolver back at the men, firing it as fast as he could and taking out one of the men. But another of them got off a shot, and the bullet hummed by Montoya's head like an angry hornet. The remaining men quickly mounted their horses and gave chase.

Antonio Barillo continued to crack the whip and shout at the team, driving the horses across the flat, dry land as fast as they could go. Inside the bouncing, fishtailing stagecoach, the four men leaned out the windows, their weapons ready. Within a few seconds, they could see the determined riders galloping after them, eating the dust that was stirred into boiling clouds by pounding hooves and whirling wheels.

Shouting at the others, John McCain said, "The riders will be hard to hit, the way this stage is bouncing! Aim for the horses!"

Soon the pursuers were drawing near, but they were now riding just two abreast directly behind the coach, making themselves difficult targets from inside the vehicle. Then, when the riders came within thirty yards of the coach, they opened fire. Though they could hardly see the attackers, McCain, Duncan, Gonzales, and Ramos started shooting, while Alonzo Montoya continued firing from up above.

When John McCain had used up all seven of his bullets in the rifle, he pulled the weapon inside and began reloading from a box of cartridges. While doing so, he shouted above the noise, "Those guerrillas are plenty clever! Notice how only the leading two fire at us until they empty their guns, and then they drop back and allow the next two to start firing!"

"And they are sure hard to hit," Manuel Ramos groaned.

As guns continued to blaze from behind them, Lucy Campbell called out from where she lay on the floor, "John, I don't understand! With all that gunfire, not one bullet has struck the coach—or at least not that I can see from down here!"

"There's a good reason for it!" McCain shouted back. "Those mangy Guatemalans want you and your parents alive because they'd have no bargaining power with the American authorities if you're dead! They obviously want their countrymen back real bad—especially President Cresada's son!"

"I wonder how they found out we were on this stage!" called out Duncan Campbell.

"They're a resourceful bunch!" replied McCain, firing

off a shot. He shook his head angrily, adding, "I sure was hoping this stagecoach idea would fool them!"

Ray Gonzales popped off two shots and then said loudly, "John, we aren't hitting a thing! We may as well save our ammunition!"

"I know," McCain mumbled, laying down his rifle and picking up a stick of dynamite. "It's time to put my alternative plan into action," he told them.

Flaring a match and crouching to protect it from the wind whistling through the swaying vehicle, McCain lit the short fuse, and the sizzle seemed a lot louder than the ear-pounding noise around them. The pursuing riders were within fifty feet of the stage, guns blazing, when McCain leaned out the window and tossed the dynamite directly in the path of the pursuers.

There was a deafening roar, and as the speeding coach pulled away from the spot of explosion, McCain watched as two riders and their horses were sent to oblivion. The attackers immediately behind them collided with the bodies and went down in a thrashing, bone-crushing heap, while the rest of the riders quickly veered around their fallen cohorts and continued their pursuit. Finally the others remounted and spurred their horses on.

The guns of their pursuers started popping again, but still no bullets struck the coach. Lucy shouted, "John, why are they shooting if they don't want to hit us?"

"They're probably hoping to frighten us into stopping," replied McCain. "When they realize it's not going to work, they'll no doubt try to get closer and shoot our horses. They'll have to go around us to do it, though, and we've got to fight back and prevent it!"

While Campbell, Ramos, and Gonzales continued firing at the galloping riders, McCain picked up another dynamite stick and lit it. The bounding coach skidded and swerved on the hard dusty ground, and although the lawman wanted to wait until the coach fishtailed a bit, giving him a clearer aim, the short fuse would not allow it.

He tossed the stick out, and just as he did so, he heard Alonzo Montoya scream up in the box.

"What happened?" McCain yelled out the window.

"Alonzo's been hit!" Antonio Barillo shouted.

The passengers all eyed each other fearfully. "Is he hurt bad?" the lawman asked.

"Yes! A bullet has ripped into his chest!" came the reply.

Suddenly Montoya's voice was heard. "I am hit bad, but I am not through!" Determination was evident in his voice as he demanded of the driver, "Hand me my shotgun!"

The shotgunner's grit became apparent when, moments later, his weapon boomed, and the charge of hot buckshot caught the lead pursuer full in the face. Watching out the window, John McCain saw a smoky red mass appear where the man's face had been, and he peeled out of the saddle. His left foot, however, caught in the stirrup, and his frightened horse veered off the road and headed across the dry, flat land, dragging the bouncing, flopping corpse.

Obviously feeling a deep sense of satisfaction, the passengers could hear Alonzo Montoya's triumphant cry in spite of his pain. But the pursuers fired back, emptying their guns at him, and Montoya's cry was cut short when a blast from one of the attacker's shotguns punched a gaping hole the size of a man's fist in the back of the Mexican's head. His shotgun clattered to the coach's roof and then sailed off and hit the ground, bouncing. The jolt dislodged the second hammer, and the weapon fired, but the charge shot into the dirt.

McCain shouted up, "Alonzo! Alonzo, are you all right?"

Again Antonio Barillo answered. In a strangled voice, he yelled, "He is dead! They killed him!"

John McCain had flared a match and was about to light the fuse when Alonzo Montoya's body fell from the box past the window. It hit the dirt, arms and legs flailing.

"Those scum!" shouted the war secretary.

Montoya's death was more than Patricia Campbell could

handle. Stiffening in her daughter's grasp, she whimpered
in abject terror. The whimper slowly built in her throat
until it became a shrill scream.

"Mother!" Lucy shouted. "Stop it! Get a grip on yourself!" The young woman seized her mother's shoulders
and shook her hard, attempting to bring her to her senses,
but Patricia's screaming stopped only long enough for her
to draw a deep, ragged breath.

When the screaming continued, Duncan Campbell leaned
over and said, "I hate to do this, but it's the only way I
know to stop hysteria." With that, he slapped his wife's
face hard. Patricia instantly fell silent, her mouth gaping,
and she looked at her husband as if she were seeing him
for the first time in her life. The strange look lasted only
seconds, and then she blinked and threw her arms around
his neck, weeping. Duncan held her tight, speaking sooth-
ing words into her ear.

John McCain was about to light the dynamite in his
hand when through the window he caught sight of four
riders ahead of the coach, coming in at them at an angle.
He cursed the Guatemalan guerrillas under his breath.
They seemed to have plenty of men and would stop at
nothing to recapture the Campbells.

Shouting at the other men in the coach, he said, "We've
got more guerrillas circling around to our left! I think
they're going to try to cut us off by getting in front of us!"

Immediately Ray Gonzales swung his rifle in that direction, waiting until they came closer to see if he could pick
them off. At the same time, John McCain flared the match
in his hand and lit the fuse of the dynamite stick he was
holding. Then another scream came from up top, just as
the fuse came alive, showering tiny sparks, and McCain
saw Antonio Barillo fall past the window and hit the ground.
The stage was now without a driver!

Suddenly the driverless stage hit a hard bump, throwing the marshal against the back of the seat. The hissing
red stick flew out of his hand and bounced to the floor

near Patricia Campbell. The secretary's wife screamed, and both Lucy and McCain scrambled to grasp it, but their heads collided, causing them both to miss it. The deadly thing rolled again, right against Patricia.

The woman screamed again, grabbing for the deadly stick, but the coach suddenly lurched again, and the dynamite rolled out of reach, bounding back toward the wide-eyed marshal. The fuse was almost burned to the end when John McCain finally grabbed it and tossed it out the window.

A rider was pulling up close and was no more than six feet from the coach when the hissing stick came out of the window, striking him square in the chest and exploding. The horrendous concussion blew both him and his horse to pieces. But unstoppable, the pursuing riders veered around the tumbling remains and continued their chase.

The stagecoach skidded and swerved behind the charging team. John McCain hollered, "I'm going to climb outside and make my way to the box. I have to take control of the horses!"

Lucy's eyes showed her fear for her man as she shouted, "Oh, John, be careful!"

Nodding, McCain reached for the door handle when he saw the four riders closing in, firing directly at the team. Suddenly the two lead horses screamed and went down, and the other four animals in the harness stumbled and fell over the bodies of their harness mates, screeching and whinnying wildly.

In the two or three seconds John McCain had to react, he threw himself on top of Lucy Campbell to protect her. The racing coach lurched, bounced hard twice, reeled, then careened and fell over in a huge cloud of dust. When it skidded to a halt on its side, the air was filled with booming guns as the attackers shot the remaining stagecoach horses.

The occupants of the overturned coach were in a jumbled heap, a tangle of arms and legs. As the passengers attempted to right themselves, they were relieved that at least no one had been seriously injured, only bruised and slightly scratched.

Patricia Campbell clung to her husband with horror etched on her pinched features. "Duncan," she moaned, "the Guatemalans have got us again!"

"I know, honey," he murmured. "But remember, they won't kill us. They need us alive so they can bargain with the authorities in New Orleans."

Patricia's voice came out in a small squeak. "But what if the authorities won't release the Guatemalans? Then we *will* be killed!"

John McCain got to his knees and helped Lucy sit up. "What are we going to do, John?" she asked fearfully.

Before McCain could respond, a sharp voice came from outside. "You in the coach! You are surrounded! If you try to fight us, you will all die! We want Secretary Campbell and his two women alive, but if there is so much as a hint of resistance, we will kill all of you! Now, climb out of there one at a time, with the Campbells coming first! If I see a weapon, my men will immediately open fire! Come out with your hands in plain sight and leave your guns in the coach!"

"Okay," McCain said to his companions with a sigh. "We have no choice but to do as the man says. We'll just have to look for a way out of this once we see what they're going to do." Giving the terrified Patricia Campbell a reassuring look while unbuckling his gun belt, McCain pleaded, "Don't give up. We're not licked yet. As long as there's breath in our lungs, we've still got a chance."

The marshal reached up and pushed the door open, and brilliant sunlight shafted through the opening. Addressing the secretary of war, McCain advised, "If you will go first, sir, I can assist the ladies up to you."

Campbell nodded, let go of his wife, and thrust himself upward through the door. McCain then helped Patricia begin the climb.

Looking up, the lawman noticed Duncan Campbell's face harden, and he presumed the secretary was assessing the attackers. He called to him, "Sir, just how many men are there?"

Campbell looked from side to side and then called down to McCain, "I'd say about a dozen. They've got the coach surrounded—and they've all got their guns drawn." His eyes flashing angrily, he reached down and pulled his wife out and then helped her to the ground.

Lucy came out next and stood beside her mother.

When U.S. Marshal John McCain emerged into the bright sunlight, one of the men took a step closer and said through a toothy grin, "You are wise not to try fighting us, *gringo*."

McCain regarded the man who seemed to be the leader coldly. He was very dark skinned—so dark, in fact, that he almost looked as though he had been burned. Thick bodied, the man's ample waist bore a double-holstered gun belt that held two bone-handled Colt .44s and a leather sheath with a silver-handled knife.

Manuel Ramos came out next and slid off the overturned vehicle, standing next to the marshal, and then finally Ray Gonzales climbed down. Focusing on the face of the blocky man who stood before him, Gonzales's mouth dropped open. "These men are not Guatemalans!" he exclaimed to McCain.

Every head in the small knot of travelers spun toward Gonzales.

"What do you mean?" demanded McCain, stunned at Gonzales's words.

"They are Mexican *banditos!* This man in front of us is Carlos Ortiz, the most infamous *bandito* in all of Mexico!"

Ortiz laughed and said, "Ah, so you know me, *señor!* Thank you for the compliment!"

John McCain eyed Ortiz with wary speculation and said, "You called the Campbells by name. You knew they were on this stage."

"That is correct, Marshal McCain," chuckled Ortiz.

Shocked further that the bandit leader also knew his name, McCain said, "How do you know who the Campbells are? And how do you know my name?"

Suddenly from behind, McCain heard a familiar voice say coldly, "I told him, Marshal McCain!"

U.S. Marshal John McCain's head snapped around, and his eyes widened in surprise. Seated on a horse was a small, dark man whose face McCain had seen many times around the Alegre Viaje Stage Line office in Chihuahua. "Rubin Lupino!" he exclaimed. "What are *you* doing here? What's going on?"

Rubin laughed maliciously and replied, "What I am doing here, Marshal, is arranging to make lots of *pesos*! Lots and lots of *pesos*! You see, this 'infamous *bandito*,' as Gonzales called Carlos Ortiz, is my second cousin. And what is going on is quite simple: We are taking the Campbells with us because I figure the Guatemalan guerrillas will pay a lot of money to get them back."

Sneering, Lupino continued, "You see, I got to thinking how the Guatemalans want the Campbells very, very bad. The next day after you had left Chihuahua, a band of guerrillas came out of the mountains to visit the mansion and find out if their countrymen had been released from the prison in New Orleans. When they found all those bodies and realized the Campbells had escaped, they were so angry they stormed into Chihuahua, trying to find out where the *norteamericanos* had gone. Right now, there are dozens of them scouring the hills and the back roads, searching for a traveling party on horseback." He paused and snickered, "You really fooled them with this stagecoach idea, Marshal McCain."

The marshal merely stared at the young assistant agent, saying nothing.

"So it came to me that I could make lots of money," Rubin Lupino went on. "After all, the guerrillas are desperate. Presidente Cresada is so fearful that he will never

see his son again—plus the other sons of Guatemalans—
that he has opened the treasury to the guerrillas for unlim-
ited expenses to carry out their mission and bring the
prisoners back. So I say to myself, 'Rubin, you can get
your hands on a fortune. You know where the Campbells
are.' "

"*Sí!*" Ortiz cut in. "When my cousin came to me where
we hide out in the mountains and told me the situation, I
could see there will be plenty of money for Rubin, my
men, and myself. I know where a guerrilla stronghold is
situated not far from my hideout, and we will stash the
Campbells in a secret place and then go to the guerrillas
and make a deal. As you can see, Señor McCain, we can
just about name our price!"

Patricia Campbell clung to her husband and cried, "Duncan, I can't go through this again! And the disgusting way
those men are looking at Lucy! I—"

"Put the Campbells on your horses, *amigos!*" Ortiz
shouted at his men, cutting off Patricia's words.

While several of the bandits strode toward Duncan Campbell and his family, Ortiz commanded a few others to
climb inside the coach and confiscate all the guns.

John McCain, Ray Gonzales, and Manuel Ramos looked
at each other helplessly. There was nothing they could do
in the face of the numerous ominous black gun muzzles
trained on them.

Patricia wailed mournfully as the bandits abruptly grabbed
her and her family, leading them roughly to their horses.

When a pair of filthy, dark hands gripped Lucy, she
looked at McCain, her face fearful and her eyes filled with
tears. Suddenly McCain's love for Lucy blinded him to
the imminent danger, and he sprang at the man holding
Lucy before any of Ortiz's men could react. Hitting the
bandit with the full force of his muscular body, McCain
broke the Mexican's hold on Lucy and the two of them hit
the ground rolling.

Tensing, Gonzales and Ramos were about to make a

move when two of the outlaws rammed guns into their backs. Immediately, they drew up short.

McCain almost had the Mexican's revolver out of its holster when two other bandits dashed to him and slammed their rifle butts down violently on his head.

The marshal went limp and lay facedown in the dirt, stunned. Shrieking his name, Lucy broke free of her captor and ran to McCain, kneeling beside him while weeping and calling his name.

The man who had seized her in the first place leapt to his feet, holstered his gun, and grabbed hold of her again. Dragging her to his horse, he hoisted her onto its back, alongside her parents, who were also now astride horses with their riders standing close by.

"John!" Lucy screamed, looking over her shoulder at his limp form lying on the ground. Then turning toward Carlos Ortiz, she screamed, "You filthy beast! If I were a man, I'd—"

"You are not a man!" bellowed Ortiz, stomping stiffly toward her. Coming beside the horse, he looked up at her and warned, "And you had best learn to control your tongue, *señorita*. Carlos Ortiz does not like to be called a filthy beast."

Lucy's tear-filled eyes were blazing. "I suppose the truth is painful to someone like you!"

The beefy Mexican drew back his hand, ready to strike her, when Duncan Campbell shouted angrily, "Don't you dare touch her!"

Ortiz stayed his hand and eyed the war secretary disdainfully. "You are in no position to give me orders, Señor Campbell."

"Look," Duncan Campbell went on in a reasonable voice, "my family and I have already been through a harrowing experience at the hands of the Guatemalan guerrillas. You've got to realize that my wife and daughter have been under indescribable strain. Why don't you just take me, and leave them here with the marshal and these other men?"

John McCain began to stir as Ortiz shook his head and said, "All three of you are going with us. There is nothing further to discuss." With that, he pivoted and made his way to where John McCain lay on the ground. Standing over him, he waited until the marshal was fully conscious and then helped him to his feet.

While McCain rubbed his aching head and gazed longingly at Lucy, Ortiz remarked, "It appears you have strong feelings for the lovely *señorita*, no?"

"I sure do," McCain replied flatly.

"Love sometimes causes a man to do foolish things, Marshal McCain—and what you just did was a foolish thing. It could have made me angry enough to have my men shoot you down like a cur dog." He smiled magnanimously, adding, "However, I admire real, genuine love, and I admire a man who will fight to protect the woman he loves. So I am going to let you live."

"But," Ortiz continued, his voice again growing harsh, "let me warn you. Do not try to follow us. I am sure that your first thought is going to be to walk to Villa Ahumada, pick up horses and guns, and come in hot pursuit, but do not even consider it. Right now, there is a chance that your lovely *señorita* will live to see you again one day . . . but if I glimpse so much as a hair of your head, she will be shot to death immediately. I can still bargain with the guerrillas with just her father and mother. Do we understand each other?"

McCain glared at Ortiz, his eyes as cold as ice. "Yeah. We understand each other."

"Good. And that goes for your friends, too. If I so much as smell any of you, the *señorita* gets a bullet in her heart."

Wrath and hatred flowed through U.S. Marshal John McCain's body, one as strong as the other. As the vile bandit leader turned and strode toward his horse, McCain vowed not only to rescue Lucy and her parents, but to make the Mexican bandit wish he had never been born.

Looking over at the young woman he loved, the lawman told her with his eyes that she should not give up hope; somehow he would find a way to overcome their captors before they were turned over to the Guatemalan guerrillas. She nodded almost imperceptibly, telling him that she understood.

Then Ortiz mounted his horse and settled his stocky frame in the saddle. As he led his men out, heading south, Lucy took a last, longing look at John McCain, who stood with his fists clenched at his sides. Then the bandits spurred their mounts, putting them into a gallop, and McCain and his comrades stood watching the line of riders until they were out of sight.

The marshal's anger was boiling over. Turning to Ray Gonzales and Manuel Ramos, McCain declared, "All right, fellas. Let's start walking. The sooner we get to Villa Ahumada and find guns and horses, the sooner we can rescue the Campbells."

"I never doubted for a moment that you would say that, John," spoke up Ray Gonzales. "But I am afraid we will never be able to catch them. By the time we can reach the town and equip ourselves, they will have had a healthy head start."

"We've got to do it," McCain countered, starting southward at a brisk pace. "Somehow, we've got to do it."

"I am all for rescuing them, Marshal," said Ramos, hurrying to keep up with the lawman's long stride. "But what about Ortiz's warning?"

"Don't worry about it," responded McCain. "I'll figure out a way to take that whole bunch by surprise. The only way Ortiz will ever deliver those people into the hands of the guerrillas is if I'm dead first—and I've got more reason to stay alive than I've ever had in my life." Glancing at his friends, he remarked, "Lucy knows I'll come after her, and I'm not going to let her down. There's more than one way to skin a cat, and that mangy cat Ortiz is going to get skinned. He's going to regret riding away with my woman and wish he'd never been—"

John McCain's words were cut off by the sudden appearance of five riders coming toward them at a fast trot over a ridge to their right. McCain stopped in his tracks, and a cold chill ran down his spine. "I guess once again I spoke too soon. Looks like we've got even more trouble."

Chapter Twelve

The riders drew closer, and U.S. Marshal John McCain could feel the tension building in his body with every passing second. Then Ray Gonzales squinted at the riders, his face showing puzzlement, and a moment later a smile broke over his rugged face. "Aha!" he exclaimed. "This is not trouble coming, John! Look! It is Rondo Ortega and four of my men!" Taking off his hat, Gonzales waved it at the oncoming riders, and Ortega and the others waved back.

John McCain breathed a silent prayer of thanks. Now they could ride fast into Villa Ahumada, equip themselves with guns and horses, and be on the trail of Ortiz and his gang.

With Ortega were men who had fought alongside John McCain at the mansion. As the riders hauled up and dismounted, there were smiles, greetings, and even embraces among the men. Smiling with relief, McCain said, "Rondo, I've never been so glad to see anybody in my life! How did this happen?"

Lifting his sombrero and scratching his head, Ortega said, "Well, it is like this. A couple of days after you left, the five of us got to talking and realized that we each had an uneasy feeling about those guerrillas who came into Chihuahua looking for the Campbells. When we learned that they sent search parties out to look for you in the back country, we figured that they might just decide to also check the main road. Since it had us worried, we decided to follow the coach to make sure you made it to Juárez all right."

Chico Gavenas spoke up. "We knew we were getting close to you when we arrived in Villa Ahumada and talked to the Alegre Viaje agent. He told us you had left a short while before. We took off at a gallop, and when we saw the dead horses and riders on the road just this side of Villa Ahumada we were sure of one thing: You had a battle on your hands."

Proceeding, Rondo Ortega said, "We drew within sight of the overturned coach just as the guerrillas were riding away with the Campbells. Before they could spot us, we quickly rode behind that ridge and hid until they were gone."

"Those men are not guerrillas," Ray Gonzales informed the newcomers quickly.

Ortega's eyebrows arched and the other men looked just as surprised. Before any of them could respond, Gonzales explained, "They are *banditos*. And their leader is Carlos Ortiz."

"Carlos Ortiz!" echoed all five at once.

"But why would Ortiz want to capture the Campbells?" queried Chico Gavenas.

His bitterness toward Rubin Lupino coloring his words, Ray Gonzales explained the situation.

Rondo Ortega was furious. "And to think I trusted that little worm!" he spat. "I cannot wait to get my hands around his scrawny neck!"

"And the sooner the better," John McCain suggested. "We can pick up guns and horses in Villa Ahumada."

"We are carrying extra guns in our saddlebags, Marshal," Ortega advised him. "But the horses we will need to get in town."

With the extra men riding double, they galloped back to Villa Ahumada, where they purchased horses, and then thundered down the road southward. They were some ten miles out of town when they spotted the Mexican bandits and their captives moving up a long slope into dense timber.

Pulling off the road behind some large boulders so as not to be seen, they watched until the procession passed from view. "Okay," McCain said, "here's my plan. Ortiz is not moving fast because he thinks he's safe. We'll circle around them so we won't be seen and get ahead of them, then set up an ambush."

"An ambush?" Gonzales asked, his brow furrowed.

"Correct," McCain replied flatly. "You heard Ortiz's warning. If he has any inkling that we're near, he'll kill Lucy. This is war, *amigos*. Ortiz declared it . . . and we're going to finish it."

Riding hard, the men made a wide circle to the west until they were well ahead of the bandits. Leaving the horses in a well-hidden thicket, they made their way through dense timber to an elevated spot beside the road where they could hide behind the trees in the deep shadows.

The column of riders was not yet in view, and John McCain turned to the others and asked, "Which of you are the best marksmen? I need two men who don't know how to miss with a rifle."

After a brief discussion it was agreed that Ray Gonzales and Chico Gavenas were the best with a rifle. McCain then explained that when the procession was directly below them, on the count of three, they would take dead aim at the heads of the men who rode double behind the Campbells. McCain would take out the man who had Lucy, Gonzales would eliminate the man who had Patricia, and Gavenas would blow away the man who had Duncan. With those bandits dead, the Campbells could hopefully maneuver their horses out of the line of fire.

"There are eight of us and eleven of them," McCain continued. "By dropping the ones riding with the Campbells, we'll immediately make it even. As soon as Ray, Chico, and I cut loose, the rest of you start shooting at the rest of them. One of you has got to be sure to get Ortiz. I'd like the privilege myself, but I'll have to forgo it for the sake of putting a bullet through the head of the mangy cur who has Lucy."

"I will get him, Marshal," volunteered Manuel Ramos.

McCain nodded, tight lipped. "Kiss him good-bye for me, will you?"

Manuel grinned. "I will let the bullet kiss him."

McCain grinned back and then peered around the tree giving him cover and saw the Mexican bandits coming down the road. "Here they come, fellas," he told them. "Ray, Chico—don't miss."

Within five minutes, the procession had neared the spot where U.S. Marshal John McCain and his Mexican friends waited, guns ready. Carlos Ortiz was in the lead with a cigar in his mouth and a look of satisfaction on his moon face. Behind Ortiz, riding single file, were the bandits who rode double with the Campbells in front of them. Duncan was first. Patricia was directly behind him, and Lucy was third. John McCain told himself the setup could not be more perfect: The Campbells were already in the saddles, which would make it easy for them to quickly ride away when the shooting started.

McCain and company took their positions, with the marshal shouldering his rifle and bracing it against the tree he hid behind. His heart pounded in his chest as he watched the procession come closer. The bandits were talking and laughing among themselves, while the Campbells looked straight ahead, their faces somber.

Manuel Ramos waited to the marshal's left, while Ray Gonzales and everyone else was to his right. As the riders slowly came into position, John McCain laid his finger against the trigger, lined the sights on the head of the swarthy man who sat behind Lucy and began a half-

whispered count as he followed the man's forward move-
ment. When he got to three, he squeezed the trigger, and
Gonzales and Gavenas were so well synchronized with
McCain that the three shots sounded as one.

Horses and riders alike were startled by the sudden
gunfire, which was followed immediately by more shots.
The first three bullets were dead on center, drilling into
the heads of the men who rode behind the Campbells,
and since their feet were not in the stirrups, the/ peeled
off the horses the instant the bullets struck, never knowing what hit them.

Though startled, the Campbells found themselves in
control of their horses and instinctively put them to a
gallop while guns roared. When they raced down the
road, out of harm's way, John McCain smiled to himself.

Manuel Ramos had hit Carlos Ortiz in the shoulder,
knocking him from the horse. While the rest of his men
either fell to gunshots or dashed for cover, the bandit
leader ran for the woods on the other side of road, clutch-
ing his wounded, bleeding shoulder. Preoccupied with
shooting it out with other bandits, Ramos did not see
Ortiz get up and run.

John McCain, however, caught a glimpse of Carlos Ortiz heading across the road. Leaving the furious gun battle
that was now ensuing as the bandits took cover and fought
back, the marshal dashed across the road, his rifle in hand.
Just before Ortiz entered the dark shadows of the dense
forest, he looked behind and saw McCain coming. Raising
his revolver, he fired twice and then plunged into the
woods. Both bullets chewed harmlessly into the dirt in
front of McCain.

Carlos Ortiz pushed deeper into the forest, and the
lawman could hear him gasping for breath—along with the
profanities he was unleashing for having missed his target.
The lawman caught sight of him leaning against a tree
some fifty yards ahead, and then Ortiz pushed himself off
and ran another fifty yards. After that, McCain lost sight of

him, meaning he was either hiding behind some cover or
had fallen flat.

Using his remarkable tracking skills, the U.S. Marshal
followed Carlos Ortiz soundlessly. Suddenly he came up
behind him and was pleased to find the corpulent Mexican
sitting on the ground facing away from him and sucking
hard for air. His back was against a tree, and his revolver
was held limp in his right hand. Finally Ortiz rolled to one
side, ready to get to his feet and stagger on. But when he
came around to the opposite side of the tree, his eyes
bulged as he found himself looking down the black muzzle
of John McCain's Winchester .44 repeater rifle. Holding
the Winchester at waist level, McCain had it trained on
Ortiz's ample belly.

McCain's voice was ice cold. "You've got a choice, Ortiz. You can drop that gun and let me take you to jail in
Juárez—or you can make a fight of it. To tell you the truth,
I hope you do the latter. Either way, I'm in a hurry to get
back to the others, so make up your mind right now. Drop
it, or use it."

McCain could see by the look in Carlos Ortiz's coal-
black eyes that he was not going to surrender. Giving the
marshal an insolent look, he thumbed back the hammer.
Even though he hated the man as much as he did, McCain
waited to be sure that he would not change his mind,
letting him bring the weapon all the way up before he
squeezed the trigger of the rifle. The Winchester bucked
in his hand and the slug ripped into Ortiz's belly. The
beefy man fell flat on his back, but still clung to his gun.
McCain worked the lever of the rifle and held it ready.
Death was already in Ortiz's glazed eyes, but he was
apparently determined to do his best to take the *gringo*
lawman with him. The revolver quivered as Ortiz once
again brought it to bear.

"You made a stupid choice," McCain remarked, and
pulled the trigger. The echo of the gunshot reverberated

through the trees, sending birds fluttering. Then it died
out and silence returned.

Carlos Ortiz lay dead with a black hole between his
bulging, sightless eyes, and it was then that John McCain
was aware that the silence was not just in the woods, there
were no more guns barking back on the road. The battle
was over. Levering another cartridge into the chamber of
the Winchester, he wheeled around and headed back,
praying that Gonzales's men had won.

Moments later, McCain neared the edge of the woods
and approached the road cautiously. Seeing the Campbells
off their horses, standing with Ray Gonzales and the others, he sighed with relief and stepped out of the trees into
the harsh sunlight.

When Lucy saw him, she broke into a run, throwing
her arms open. "John!" she cried. "Oh, John!"

McCain dropped the rifle and embraced her, and she
clung to him and wept. After a few moments, the young
woman laid her head against his chest and declared breathlessly, "I knew you'd come, darling! I knew you'd figure
out a way to rescue us!"

"I'm glad you knew you could count on me." McCain
held her a few more moments and then suggested, "Let's
go."

The marshal picked up the rifle, and then he and Lucy
walked over to join the others. As they drew up, he
looked at a horse that had a dead man draped over its
back. Darting his eyes from face to face, he quickly ascer-
tained that Armundo Furatado was missing from the group—
and it was he who was draped over the horse.

Ray Gonzales explained that Armundo had taken a bullet in the heart, while Roberto Mendez had been nicked
in the left arm, but the wound was not serious. All of the
bandits were dead, including Rubin Lupino. Their bodies
were lying up amid the trees.

Manuel Ramos then asked, "What about Ortiz, Marshal? I thought I hit him, since I saw him fall off his horse

after I fired, but another bandit was shooting at me and I
had to take care of him."

"You did hit him, Manuel," replied McCain. "Got him
in the left shoulder. He was bleeding like a stuck pig
when I caught up with him." He sniffed derisively, adding, "I guess you might say I put him out of his misery."

"You killed him?" asked Duncan Campbell, who looked
slightly dazed by the whole experience.

"Yes, sir. Though it went against my grain, I gave him a
chance to surrender—but he didn't take it. He tried to kill
me, so I took him out."

The war secretary shook his head. "Well, it doesn't
surprise me—nor does it sadden me in any way that he's
dead. John, I can't thank you and your companions enough
for coming after us. There's no telling what might have
happened if you hadn't."

Shrugging, the lawman replied modestly, "It's my job,
sir." Then he gave Lucy a quick glance and grinned. "Of
course, I *did* have an extra incentive."

All the survivors returned to Villa Ahumada, leaving
Armundo Furatado's body with the local undertaker for
burial. They were given a new team of horses by the
Alegre Viaje agent, who also transported the travelers
back to the overturned stagecoach in a wagon while Ortega and his three companions followed on their horses.
The vehicle was righted, and the travelers were once
again on their way to Juárez. Ray Gonzales drove, and
Manuel Ramos rode shotgun. John McCain rode inside
the coach with the Campbells, while Rondo Ortega and
Gonzales's three remaining men escorted the coach on
horseback.

It was one o'clock in the afternoon the next day when
the dusty Alegre Viaje stagecoach pulled into Juárez and
halted at the stage office. John McCain got permission
from the agent to take the coach across the Rio Grande so

the Campbells would not have to walk across the bridge to El Paso, and the coach was soon heading northward.

McCain leaned back in the seat and said, "Well, folks, your journey across Mexico is over."

Lucy sighed and then declared wryly, "Yes, and I think they ought to rename the Alegre Viaje company. Our journey wasn't very joyful—although, to be fair, it wasn't the company's fault."

As the coach rolled over the bridge that spanned the lazy Rio Grande, McCain told the others, "We'll head for the railroad depot first and find out when the next eastbound train is leaving. Once we know that, we can decide where you'll stay until departure time."

Lucy Campbell's eyes showed sudden sadness, and she slipped her hand inside the crook of John's arm and held on tight. The handsome lawman patted her hand, although he, too, felt the pang of their impending separation.

Duncan Campbell smiled at McCain and remarked, "I'm going to talk to the President, John. There should be some kind of special commendation conferred upon you for a job well done."

McCain's face reddened. "That isn't necessary, sir. It's reward enough just to know you and the ladies are safe from the Guatemalans—and as I said, I was merely doing my job."

Campbell smiled again, declaring, "You're far too modest." Then he mused, "I assume you and Lucy are going to keep in touch . . . see each other again."

Looking into her blue eyes, John answered, "As a matter of fact, I want to talk to Lucy about that, sir."

Lucy Campbell looked at him tenderly and gave him a soft, sweet smile.

Arriving at the depot, they were surprised to learn that an eastbound train was leaving in less than an hour. It had no Pullman coach or private compartments, but when they changed trains at Dallas, they could get more comfortable accommodations for the remainder of the trip to

Washington. The Campbells purchased their tickets, and the war secretary asked McCain if he would wire Washington and advise the President that they were safe and on their way home.

After assuring him he would take care of it, McCain took Lucy's arm, and leaving the others in the depot, he led her outside to talk privately. They made their way to a bench on the platform and sat down. The train sat on the track a few feet away, the engine sending out puffs of white steam, and people were already boarding.

Taking Lucy's hand in his own, John McCain told her above the noise of the bustling crowd, "Time is short, so there's no time to work up to this. I'll just have to ask it flat out." He looked deeply into the eyes studying his own and asked, "Lucy, will you marry me?"

The sudden proposal obviously took the beautiful blonde by surprise. Overwhelmed, she merely stared at him for a moment and then asked, "How . . . how soon do you want to get married?"

"Right away. I've got some money saved, and—"

"John," she interrupted, "I . . . well, I know without a shadow of a doubt that I am in love with you, but . . . but—"

"But what?"

"Well, it's just that . . . well, marriage is the biggest step in life, and with all that's happened, I need more time to consider it. I . . . need a little time to settle down. Would you give me that, John? We can write to each other and get to know each other better. Then we can approach the marriage question and—"

"There's no question with me," cut in McCain. "But because I want you to be absolutely certain, I will bow to your wishes."

"It'll work out, darling," she told him softly. "But everything has happened so fast. Besides, I believe in that old adage: Absence makes the heart grow fonder."

The bell on the big engine began to clang and the conductor called out, "All aboard! All aboard!"

"Well, I know that my love for you will grow every day," he said, standing and helping her up. "Write me in care of the U.S. marshal's office in Austin."

"You'll answer right back?"

"Sure," he promised and took her in his arms.

They kissed and then walked to the train, where Lucy's parents were about to board. Gonzales and the others stood with them, and fond good-byes were said. Then the young couple briefly kissed again, and Lucy had tears in her eyes as she stepped onto the train ahead of her parents. Following alongside the car, McCain watched Lucy's progress down the aisle until she found a seat by the window. Her parents sat in the seats behind her.

Staring out at John McCain's handsome face, Lucy felt as though her heart were breaking. She glanced up as two swarthy men walked into the car and then looked out the window again, only peripherally aware that the pair had sat down directly behind Duncan and Patricia Campbell.

Suddenly her blood turned to ice as she heard the voice of one of the men softly tell her father, "We are Guatemalan guerrillas, and this is a gun pressed against your back, Señor Campbell. My *compadre* has one pointed at your *esposa*, and if you try to call for help, we will kill your wife and daughter. We have two men near the front of the train, and once it is out of El Paso, they will take over the engine and stop it—and you will once again be our prisoners!"

The conductor stood on the steps of the Campbell's car and called out a final, "All aboard! All aboard!"

Marshal John McCain pressed his face close to the window and shouted, "I love you, darling!"

But Lucy did not respond in kind. Rather, her eyes were panic stricken, and she silently mouthed the word,

"Guatemalans." Then she inclined her head in the direction of the seats behind.

Following her cues, McCain saw the two swarthy men seated behind the Campbells, one of whom was speaking to the war secretary. The lawman felt a cold ball form in his stomach, but he backed away casually, acting as if he were leaving. He waved to Lucy and then hurried along the platform to the conductor. The trainman was about to signal the engineer to pull out.

McCain told him urgently, "Don't let the train leave, sir! I am a United States marshal, and I've got to apprehend two men who have just boarded!"

The conductor's face lost color. "Yes, Marshal. I'll hold it."

McCain's Mexican friends had retreated a short distance away to let the lawman have his private good-bye with Lucy. When the marshal waved at them to join him, they came on the run, apparently reading his face and realizing something was wrong.

"What is it, John?" queried Ray Gonzales.

"There are a pair of Guatemalan guerrillas seated behind Mr. and Mrs. Campbell on the train," McCain replied. "If too many of us go in there, it could arouse their suspicions. So, Ray, you and I will board while the rest of you keep your eyes open. There may be more of them close by."

While the others waited, ready to go into action, John McCain and Ray Gonzales walked along the platform and stepped into the rear of the half-filled car. McCain was glad to see that no one was seated directly behind the two guerrillas, and he whispered to Gonzales, "We'll take those vacant seats behind them. Walk normally, and don't pull your gun until after you sit down. Then cock the hammer just as you place the muzzle at the back of your man's neck so he'll hear it. I'll do the talking."

Gonzales nodded and walked quickly toward the designated seat.

McCain followed Gonzales and sat down, pulling his gun. The guerrilla in front of McCain was still leaning forward, talking to the war secretary, and although he had a revolver pressed against the back of Campbell's seat, the marshal could see it was not cocked. The same thing was true of the other man holding his gun against the back of Patricia's seat.

Looking at Gonzales, the marshal nodded and placed his gun against the back of the guerrilla's head. Gonzales did the same thing, and then the hammers were thumbed back simultaneously, making their ominous clicks. Both guerrillas immediately stiffened at the sound.

McCain's voice was steady and cold. "If either of you so much as twitches an ear, you're dead. Drop your guns on the floor."

Almost in unison, both revolvers clattered to the floor, while several of the passengers, seeing what was happening, screamed in alarm.

McCain loudly identified himself, assuring the passengers that no harm would come to them. He then instructed, "Everybody get out of the car. Mr. and Mrs. Campbell, you and Lucy leave as well." When the car was empty, the lawman ordered, "All right, you two. Stand up real slow and lace your fingers behind your heads, then step away from your seats."

McCain and Gonzales held the guerrillas at gunpoint as they slowly obeyed the marshal's commands. But the moment they stepped into the aisle, they glanced at each other and lunged at their captors.

One of them tried to grab McCain's gun, but the seasoned lawman was too fast, and he fired point blank into the guerrilla's midsection. He collapsed, eyes bulging. The other guerrilla briefly grasped Ray Gonzales's gun hand, but Gonzales twisted it free and then brought the barrel of his revolver savagely down on the man's head, crushing his skull. He went down in a heap, dead.

McCain's man was lying in the aisle with blood pumping from the gaping hole in his stomach. The conductor appeared just as the guerrilla breathed his last and died.

Rushing back into the car, Duncan Campbell exclaimed excitedly, "John, those men said there are two more guerrillas somewhere near the front of the train who are planning on taking it over!"

Looking at the conductor, McCain ordered, "Take care of these corpses, will you?" Even as he spoke, he was hurrying through the coach with Ray Gonzales at his heels. They stepped onto the platform, and McCain only had time to give Lucy a reassuring smile as he signaled to Rondo Ortega and the other Mexicans to follow him.

As he started toward the front of the train, John McCain saw two swarthy men standing on the steps of the first passenger car a hundred feet ahead, looking in his direction. The lawman was sure they were the Guatemalans. They apparently had heard the shot and come out of the car to investigate it, knowing that their *compadres* were further back on the train, trying to carry out their kidnap attempt.

When the guerrillas saw McCain and the Mexicans running toward them, guns in hand, they turned, climbed the steps onto the train, and disappeared. Moments later McCain reached the spot where they had been. Standing on the platform, he looked first in the passenger car and then in the mail car. Then movement caught his eye outside, and he spotted the two guerrillas running across the railroad yards in the direction of the river.

Bounding over the platform to the other side of the train, the marshal called for his companions to follow. Hopping tracks and running hard, the Guatemalans darted between freight cars and toolsheds, apparently heading for the road—and from there to the bridge that crossed into Mexico.

As John McCain ran for all he was worth, he saw that the direction in which the guerrillas were headed was taking them toward an empty freight car sitting on a side track that was being repaired by a crew of men. McCain shouted to the railroad workers, "Hey! Stop those men! I'm a U.S. marshal! Stop those men!"

The workers' heads came up, and they stared after the Guatemalans, who pulled their guns while they ran and then changed course so as to avoid going near the workers. But the rough and rugged railroad men, two of whom held crowbars, started running after the guerrillas, who were only some forty feet away.

When the guerrillas saw the workers coming after them, they fired on the run, but their bullets went wild. The two railroad men who had the crowbars spoke quickly to each other and suddenly halted. They swung the metal bars around their heads to gain momentum, then let them loose. Both crowbars sailed through the air, and one hit its target square on the back of the neck, knocking him down. The other metal bar dropped low, striking the second guerrilla behind the knees. He stumbled and rolled on the ground.

By the time the guerrillas could collect themselves and bring their guns to bear, John McCain was beside them. The marshal aimed his revolver and commanded, "Drop those guns!"

But surrender apparently was not in their makeup, and they brought their guns up to fire. McCain's Colt .45 roared, sending one of the Guatemalans into eternity with a bullet through his heart. Before the lawman could thumb back the hammer for another shot, the Mexicans killed the other guerrilla, each putting a bullet in him.

Thanking the workers for their help, U.S. Marshal John McCain and his loyal companions walked quickly back to the train. Because of the excitement, the conductor had held up its departure, and when McCain and his friends returned to the depot platform, the Campbells were waiting beside the car with the conductor. To make sure the train was free of any additional guerrillas, McCain and the Mexicans went through every car. Alighting from the last coach, they hurried back to the Campbells and assured them they were now safe. After once again expressing their heartfelt gratitude for all McCain and his friends had done, the war secretary and his wife reboarded the train.

The delay gave John McCain and Lucy Campbell the opportunity for another farewell. Folding her in his arms, the lawman kissed her, and she repeated her words of love and promised to write soon. He waited while she climbed back into the car and took the window seat as before and then stood on the platform waving as the train chugged away.

The Mexicans flanked the heavy-hearted U.S. marshal, and Ray Gonzales remarked, "You are a lucky man, John."

"That I am," McCain agreed with a sigh, watching the train slowly leave the station.

"Are you going to get married?" Gonzales queried.

"We are," replied McCain. "But she needs a little time before we actually set the date."

The caboose finally rolled away, and McCain was about to turn away when, to his utter surprise, he saw a young woman standing on the opposite side of the tracks—a young woman with long, blond hair, big sky-blue eyes, and a smile that lit up the darkest night.

"Lucy!" gasped the stunned lawman, realizing she had jumped off the slow-moving train after her window had passed from his view.

Leaping off the platform, McCain ran to her and folded her into his arms. The young woman whispered in his ear, "Is that proposal still good?"

"It sure is!" McCain exclaimed, holding her even tighter. "But . . . I thought you said you needed more time—plus something about absence making the heart grow fonder."

Pulling back so she could look him in the eyes, Lucy caressed his cheek and said, "I *did* take more time. It's been all of twenty minutes since I said that. And . . . being apart those moments before I could step off the train was enough time to make me love you even more."

U.S. Marshal John McCain stood mute with joy, hardly able to believe what was happening. Gripping his hands with her own, Lucy told him, "Father and Mother said to tell you they would be expecting us on the next train to Washington. They'll begin preparations immediately for the wedding. Can you get the time off?"

Elated beyond description, John McCain chuckled and replied, "After the trip I just took to Chihuahua, I've got some time coming!"

"Oh, John," Lucy sighed, "I'm so very, very happy!"

John McCain's strong arms enfolded her once again. While the Mexicans on the platform whistled loudly and Ray Gonzales imitated the mournful howl of a wolf calling for its mate, the couple's lips blended in a long, tender kiss.

★ WAGONS WEST ★

This continuing, magnificent saga recounts the adventures of a brave
band of settlers, all of different backgrounds, all sharing one dream—
to find a new and better life.

☐	26822	**INDEPENDENCE! #1**	$4.50
☐	26162	**NEBRASKA! #2**	$4.50
☐	26242	**WYOMING! #3**	$4.50
☐	26072	**OREGON! #4**	$4.50
☐	26070	**TEXAS! #5**	$4.50
☐	26377	**CALIFORNIA! #6**	$4.50
☐	26546	**COLORADO! #7**	$4.50
☐	26069	**NEVADA! #8**	$4.50
☐	26163	**WASHINGTON! #9**	$4.50
☐	26073	**MONTANA! #10**	$4.50
☐	26184	**DAKOTA! #11**	$4.50
☐	26521	**UTAH! #12**	$4.50
☐	26071	**IDAHO! #13**	$4.50
☐	26367	**MISSOURI! #14**	$4.50
☐	27141	**MISSISSIPPI! #15**	$4.50
☐	25247	**LOUISIANA! #16**	$4.50
☐	25622	**TENNESSEE! #17**	$4.50
☐	26022	**ILLINOIS! #18**	$4.50
☐	26533	**WISCONSIN! #19**	$4.50
☐	26849	**KENTUCKY! #20**	$4.50
☐	27065	**ARIZONA! #21**	$4.50
☐	27458	**NEW MEXICO! #22**	$4.50
☐	27703	**OKLAHOMA! #23**	$4.50
☐	28180	**CELEBRATION! #24**	$4.50